Devoted Sinner

Damaged Devils #6

Charity Parkerson

Punk & Sissy Publications

Copyright

—Warning: This book is intended for readers over the age of 18. Some of my books contain allusions to past abuse and trauma.

Editor: BZ Hercules & Consultants

Cover art: Temptation Creations

Contents

Author Note

THIS IS A DARK romance series filled with possible triggers. If you need a list, you can skip to the content warning after the About the Author page or check my website: charityparkerson.com/damaged-devils

Introduction

King sees working for Bryson as punishment. Bryson sees it as winning.

Working for Bryson isn't by choice. As one of the many men trained by an underground organization to be an assassin, King has simply been sold to the highest bidder. His job is to keep Bryson safe. Even though he has nothing against Bryson, a slave is a slave, and King is tired of this life. That doesn't stop his immediate attraction, which grows stronger every day. Thankfully, King is used to going unnoticed.

While Bryson truly needs King's protection, that's not the biggest reason he brought King to live with him. He spent a lot of time with King's former boss. He knows King isn't safe there. Plus, Bryson enjoys pretty things, and he's not above using every trick to collect them. Unfortunately, months of watching King has become an obsession. It doesn't matter if they feel the same way. There's still someone out there wanting him dead. Neither of them will be free as long as they're always wondering if the other one is there because they have to be.

Devoted Sinner is the sixth book in Charity Parkerson's Damaged Devils series. These are dark romance stories with crime lords, assassins, and sociopaths who find their hearts. They are best enjoyed when read in order.

Chapter One

Ten months. That was how long Bryson had King living under his roof. Two years. That was how long Bryson had craved him. He supposed that seemed downright pathetic. Maybe it was, but King was new territory for Bryson. As someone on the list of the richest men in the world, he was accustomed to having whatever he wanted. There was no one who didn't have a price. If someone thought they couldn't be bought, they simply hadn't been handed the right amount of zeros yet. In fact, he had purchased King from his previous owner. After over a year of watching King from afar, he had bought out King's contract and doubled his salary. Bryson truly needed the guard's services. There was someone out there trying to kill him. But there was always someone out there ready to kill him and Bryson never really sweated that. He had wanted King under his roof where Bryson could watch him, dream, and brood.

Truth be told, while Bryson had taken part in countless sexual escapades where several people had been involved at one time—men and women—he had never been one on one with another man. There was just something about King. For the past ten months, since he had brought King to live with him, Bryson had fruitlessly hoped King would return his interest. Instead, King simply did his job. It was maddening.

Bryson stroked his bottom lip and watched King. He adored the way the man's dark hair framed his face. Occasionally, his whiskey-colored eyes would focus on Bryson. Each and every time, even after two years of knowing him, butterflies stirred in Bryson's stomach.

"What would you like me to do with this, boss? Should I alert the authorities?"

Bryson shook himself from his non-stop daydreaming. He forced his gaze to the note King held. It was just two words: *You're dead*. "No. There's no point. They'll just tell me they're looking into it and that I should hire more security. Just add it to the stack of threatening letters I've received in the past year. If nothing else, if this person ever shows themselves, we'll have a case built for the useless police."

King nodded and crossed the room to the filing cabinet. Bryson watched the sexy way King's huge body moved. He had a light, graceful walk for such a big guy. King filed the note away with the rest.

"Would you like to go out for dinner tonight?"

King glanced his way. "As always, it's up to you. It's my job to follow."

Bryson ground his back teeth. There it was, the thing that drove him insane. King never let him forget Bryson owned him. He never shared an opinion or lost his professionalism for a second. King was completely unmoved by Bryson in every way. Bryson had never had to work this hard. Sometimes, he thought—maybe—that was the appeal, but no. Bryson knew better. He was obsessed with the man.

Bryson stood. "Very well. If it's up to me, then I think I'm in the mood to spoil someone."

King showed no reaction. "Should I tell your son to get ready?"

A smile spread across Bryson's lips. He enjoyed keeping King on his toes. "There's no need. He left an hour ago to go out with friends. You know how it is. He's young and trying to squeeze in as much time with his friends as he can before he leaves for college."

"No. I don't actually know how it is."

Bryson shook his head at King's deadpan response. "Come on. Let's go buy things."

King nodded and followed on Bryson's heels to the back door. "Where would you like to go first?" King reached past Bryson and opened the door to the garage for him.

Bryson headed for his Lykan Hyper-Sport. He knew how much King enjoyed driving it. "You choose. Get behind the wheel and take me where you like to shop."

King opened the passenger side door for Bryson. He didn't respond until after he was behind the wheel and the car purred to life. "I'm your employee. It's best if you decide."

A loud sigh escaped Bryson before he could stop it. He leaned his head back against the seat and stared at King's profile. There had to be a way to crack King's shell. Bryson would figure it out one day.

"I have to be honest with you. Sometimes, I get downright sick of making decisions. Can you take it this one time? You choose where we shop and where we eat. I insist."

King's lips parted, as if he meant to argue. Then he looked resigned and backed from the garage.

Bryson hid a smile. He didn't look away from King. "Tell me something about yourself," he said the moment King was on the road.

"There's nothing to tell."

Bryson rolled his eyes. "You're what? Thirty-five? You've only been with me ten months. There's a lot of life before that to talk about."

King shrugged. "Not really."

It was like pulling teeth. "Tell me about your childhood."

King snorted. "Absolutely not."

Okay. Partly, that was fair. Bryson knew King had been raised in an assassin program and trained to be sold to people like Bryson. But surely the man had a life before that. As far as Bryson knew, this society of assassins hadn't taken kids from birth. He had to have been at least twelve or so before his life changed. "Who were you before the society? How old were you when you joined the program? How did you end up there?"

A slight smile touched King's lips. Bryson's breath caught. He really liked King. "Joined the program," King said, repeating Bryson's words and sounding thoughtful. "That's a nice way of saying they bought me from an orphanage."

"You were an orphan?" Bryson knew he sounded dumb, but he wanted King to keep talking.

"Not originally. I had parents. A pastor for a father and his obedient wife. The moment they realized I hadn't turned out the way they expected, that I was a sinner, they tossed me aside."

"I can't imagine anything my son could do to make me toss him aside." Bryson was thoroughly horrified. He genuinely tried to think of anything at all that Kylian could do that would make him give him up, and there was literally nothing. Even if his son turned out to be a serial killer, he couldn't stop loving him.

King looked his way while they were stopped at a light. He held Bryson's stare. "That's because you're a good person and a good father. Not everyone is, and that's doubly true for the people who often try to claim the most values. They think church gives them absolution in everything they do outside of that building."

"I can't imagine anyone not being proud of you."

The light turned green. King looked away. "Like I said, you're a good person."

Bryson wasn't so sure that was true. He took money from bad people and helped them achieve bad things. Bryson kept King with him when all he had to do was set him free. He assuaged his guilt by telling himself he paid King handsomely. But in his heart, he still understood King wasn't free. Bryson held the contract on his life. If he left, all Bryson had to do was tell King's former boss, Archer, and King would disappear permanently. Bryson would never do that, but he also hadn't set King free despite the money being nothing to him. He told himself—in a way—he kept King safe. King had seen too much. There were people who would never let him live if he left Bryson's care. But, in the end, none of that mattered because the truth still existed. King was a slave. That meant he would never be free to love Bryson.

Two years ago, King had met Bryson while working for someone else. He had dealings with King's old boss. From the day they met, King felt Bryson's gaze on him. His amber stare followed King's every move. With anyone else, he might have been uncomfortable. King didn't feel that way with Bryson. Of everyone King had ever served, Bryson was the kindest. That was the only reason King humored him by speaking at all. He didn't owe anyone his words or thoughts. They might own him, but no one would ever own his mind. He chose who saw that.

King drove to a high-end mall in the center of Massachusetts. While he did some shopping there occasionally, his real goal was to head to one of the many restaurants inside. It was his favorite, and he'd never been there with Bryson before. He wasn't sure if Bryson didn't know the place existed, didn't like it, or simply hadn't taken King. Either way, Bryson had insisted King choose, so they were going.

After finding a spot in the parking garage, King circled the car and opened the door for Bryson. He held out his hand to help Bryson out of the car. It was a habit. They were both big guys, and it was a small car low to the ground. Plus, he liked it when Bryson touched him. King didn't get a lot of human contact.

Bryson's palm slid across his. Sometimes, King wondered if Bryson enjoyed these moments too. Unfortunately, despite the way he watched King, King had a sneaking suspicion Bryson was straight. He hadn't dated in the ten months King had been with him. King thought maybe he was a workaholic. Otherwise, he didn't know why Bryson always stayed home unless he was working or going somewhere with King. The man had a son and an ex-wife. He could be bisexual, but King doubted it. King chalked up any attraction on his behalf to being touch starved. Otherwise, they had nothing in common.

When Bryson released King's hand, King fought a wave of disappointment. Again, touch starved. He couldn't help it. King closed the door. Together, they headed inside the mall.

"What's your favorite store here?"

King hadn't expected to immediately admit to it being a restaurant that drew him here. Here they were, though. "Actually, this place has my favorite restaurant."

Bryson's sexy smile swung his way. "Really? You've been with me for almost a year, and you never said a thing. We've been out to eat countless times."

King shrugged. "You're the boss. We go where you want."

Bryson's smile faltered. "You're allowed to have an opinion too. You're not a prisoner, and I value your thoughts. In fact, I'd go as far as to say we're friends." He looked uncomfortable for a moment. "At least, you're my friend." Bryson's expression turned somewhat hurt. "How pathetic, honestly. The only friend I have is someone I pay to be with me." Bryson's pace quickened, as if he didn't want King to look at him any longer. King let him have his space.

When they reached the elevator, King reached past Bryson to push the button, calling for the lift. He spoke close to Bryson's ear as he pressed the button. "You're my friend. That has nothing to do with you paying me." It was somewhat true. They were friends insomuch as they could be with Bryson knowing next to nothing about him.

Bryson turned his head. Their faces were inches apart. Neither of them moved. Bryson's eyes were twice as beautiful up close. That adorable brown curl that always clung to his forehead and refused to behave made King want to touch it. The door opened, breaking the spell. King leaned away, waiting until Bryson climbed inside the elevator so he could physically protect his back.

King kept his gaze straight ahead as he hit the button, taking them upstairs. They held their silence as the elevator door opened inside the mall. They stepped out. King kept his gaze moving, searching for any threats.

"While I fully expect to experience this restaurant with you, tell me where you like to shop."

The question made King uncomfortable. There were stores there where he shopped, but Bryson wouldn't understand why. King motioned helplessly toward a nearby store. Bryson headed that way. They had to pass a posted security guard to get inside. All the stores in this mall were like that. Everything inside cost more than some people's rent.

Bryson immediately headed for the men's section. King watched his back. Bryson stopped at a rack and started fingering through the clothes. King glanced around. A pink cashmere sweater caught King's eye. He glanced Bryson's way. Bryson was still preoccupied. King took a chance and felt of the sweater. It was as soft as it looked. He doubted they had one in his size since it was meant for women. Still, he might have to come back later alone and check.

Before he released the sweater, Bryson caught him. They held each other's stare. King released the top. His mind raced.

"It's soft." Even to his ears, he sounded guilty.

Bryson moved to the sweater and felt of it. “Damn. It really is. Why do women get all the cozy shit?”

King shrugged. “There’s nothing stopping you from wearing it. Clothing doesn’t have a gender.” He had no idea why he said that. King should have let it go.

To his relief, Bryson nodded. “That’s true.” Bryson moved on and grabbed a pink dress shirt. He held it up to King and eyed him. “Pink is your color, I think. Why don’t you wear it?”

He did. Just not around Bryson. King had another life. One very few people knew about. Instead of answering, King shrugged again.

Bryson put the shirt back and moved back to the pink sweater. He flipped through the sizes until he found the largest one. Bryson held it against King's chest. "I think this would fit you. It would likely show your midriff." Bryson's gaze moved to hold King's stare. "That would be okay, though."

King couldn't look away. For a second, he swore Bryson knew his secret. King also hadn't been as attracted to anyone as he was in that moment. "I'd wear it."

"Good." Bryson kept the sweater and moved along. King wondered how much of this torment he could stand.

The way King had held his stare. Fuck. Bryson needed the sweater to hide his erection. King didn't look like the type to get fucked. He probably expected to be the one doing the fucking, and while Bryson didn't think he would be into that, King had him questioning a lot of things. He bought King the sweater. Bryson also grabbed one in black when King was busy looking out for danger. Bryson handed the bag to King as they walked out the door.

"Here, you'll look fantastic."

King accepted the bag. "Thank you." He sounded uncomfortable. Too bad.

Bryson wasn't finished. He headed inside a cosmetics store.

"I need some new cologne. What's your favorite?"

King's eyes moved from side to side like he might run. "I don't know."

Bryson sighed. "Very well. You leave me no choice." He headed for the perfumes, pretending to be confused. "I can never find anything in this store."

With a huff, King snagged the back of his shirt and turned him toward the unisex section. "This one," he said gruffly, pointing toward one.

Bryson snagged it and sprayed King. He leaned in and sniffed. "You're right. That's perfect for you." He handed the salesperson following them his credit card. In no time, King carried his new sweaters and scent.

Next, Bryson made his way inside the closest high-end store for handbags. “You know, I’ve never understood why men aren’t allowed to carry purses. They’re so convenient.”

“Who says men can’t carry purses?”

Bryson hid a triumphant smile at King’s bitter tone. He slowly pulled King from his shell. Bryson grabbed a brown leather crossbody bag and draped it across King’s chest. He eyed his work and nodded. “Yes. This would be perfect for that sweater.” He immediately handed off his card before King could argue. Then they were on their way. “What else do you need?”

He heard King take a breath. Bryson wondered if he should stop. He wanted King to be real with him, but he worried he might go too far too fast. Bryson quickly gave King an out just in case. "Or would you rather eat?"

King's shoulders relaxed. "Please?"

Bryson looked away and smirked. He would do a lot to hear King beg. The restaurant turned out to be perfect. It had low lighting and intimate tables. King and Bryson were forced to sit so close, their feet kept brushing beneath the table. Since King had demanded a corner table where he could keep his back against the wall and see the entire room, they were seated in an area where they were the only customers. King kept his gaze moving. Bryson stared at King.

Occasionally, King would meet his gaze before going back to eyeing the room. The intimacy of the moment made Bryson say things he shouldn't. "Do I make you nervous?"

King met his stare. "No. Why?"

Bryson shrugged. "I know you're doing your job by keeping watch, but sometimes I get the feeling you're also avoiding my gaze."

A slow, sexy smirk touched King's lips. "I'm not easily spooked."

Their server appeared, interrupting their moment.

Bryson motioned for King to order. "Choose for me. It's still your day to take decisions off my hands."

King's smile turned adorable, making Bryson's heart skip a beat. "Okay. No complaints if you don't like my choices."

"Fair enough."

King ordered.

Bryson didn't hear a word of it. He was too busy watching the way King's lips moved. Maybe he was bored. With Bryson's money, he had tried almost everything twice. Before King, he had never wanted to give a man a whirl. But fuck, he couldn't stop imagining King in that sweater. He wanted to smell like that cologne, but not from wearing it. He wanted to wear King.

The server walked away, and King focused on him again. "Is that okay?"

Bryson chuckled. "I wasn't listening."

Another heart-stopping smile snapped to King's lips. "Your attention isn't easily held, is it?"

That wasn't true. Bryson hadn't wanted to focus on anything else for two years. King had his full attention. He couldn't say that. "Some things hold my interest more than others."

King held his stare and Bryson knew he wasn't oblivious, but Bryson enjoyed keeping him off balance.

"What are your thoughts on corsets?"

King blinked. "What?"

"Corsets," Bryson repeated. "You said clothing isn't gendered, and it got me to thinking. A few things feel gendered—like bras and corsets."

To his delight, King didn't bow out of the conversation. "I've seen a lot of extremely stunning men wear bras and corsets."

Bryson nodded, intentionally looking thoughtful. "Good to know. We'll look at corsets after dinner."

King shook his head, but a sexy smile played on his lips as he went back to keeping an eye out for danger. One of these days, Bryson would crack him. It was only a matter of time.

Chapter Two

The night with Bryson had been low-key amazing. While King had always known Bryson was worth protecting, he hadn't truly realized how much he enjoyed Bryson's company until he had Bryson's full attention. He hadn't wanted their time to end, but everything did eventually.

Each Friday night, King was off duty, and he didn't return to duty until late Sunday night. Of course, Bryson and he always crossed paths throughout the weekends. They still lived together, after all. But Bryson wasn't his responsibility on the weekends and King needed space to be himself.

He always waited until the house fell silent to transform. Tonight, he needed to try on the clothes Bryson bought him first. The corset was amazing. While King had owned corsets in the past, they were always a lower quality since he had to buy them on the sly. Once he had the corset in place sans shirt, he couldn't help himself. He knew exactly which pair of fishnets and leather skirt would go with it. King pulled on a thong before the stockings. From there, he added a black leather skirt that barely hid his ass cheeks. He turned in front of the full-length mirror, taking in the whole picture. King loved it. No one understood how much he adored these moments. Even though King understood he could never freely live this way, he still treasured the freedom when he could.

Only one friend had ever known about King. King rubbed his chest at the thought. He hadn't seen Nebraska in two months, since Nebraska's wedding. King missed trying on outfits for Nebraska—like a fashion show. He wished Nebraska was here tonight to give his opinion before King sneaked away to his club. It was hard being invisible. King picked the new perfume Bryson bought him and sprayed himself. It was doubly hard knowing he would never be loved like this. Even if he was a free man, the likelihood of being accepted as is was slim to none. He was an oddity.

Determined to hang on to the joy of new clothes, King grabbed his eye liner and went to work on his eyes. He would keep it simple tonight. The outfit screamed for dark liner and nothing else. Next, he found a pair of black combat boots. With the boots in hand, he silently headed for the door. While Bryson never came out of his bedroom after turning in for the night, King couldn't take any chances. He checked the hall and then tiptoed from the room. Once he made it to the garage and his car, he would be home free. King made it to the living room before a sound had him freezing in his tracks. His ears strained and his gaze darted to every corner of the room. In the darkness, nothing stirred. The open curtains allowed the security lights to cast a glow across the floor. It hit King. The security lights had been triggered. Before he had time to investigate, a shadow crossed the light, perfectly outlining someone holding a gun.

"I heard a noise."

King's chin shot up at Bryson's whisper. Then a sound he had heard countless times had some form of sixth sense kicking in. King dropped his boots and ran full speed at Bryson. Just as he tackled the man to the floor, the gunfire began. Glass, wood, and debris flew in every direction. King tried making himself bigger to protect Bryson. He covered Bryson's head and face. Glass cut into his skin in several places. Finally, two pops sounded. The rapid gunfire fell silent. Two more pops rang out before everything went still.

King lifted his head. His gaze swept Bryson's body. He searched for any sign he was hurt. "Are you okay?"

Bryson nodded. "Are you?"

King took stock. "I only took some glass, I think."

They held each other's stare. Neither of them moved.

"Sir, the threat has been neutralized."

The comment from the doorway, coming from the weekend security team, pulled King from his trance. Horror washed over him as he recalled how he was dressed.

"Thank you. Please take care of things," Bryson called toward the door, sounding surprisingly calm.

"Yes, sir."

When they were alone again, Bryson went back to holding King's stare. "Stand up and let me see."

Shock had King slow to move. That and he dreaded the moment Bryson fully saw him. He winced as he moved to his feet and several shards of glass made themselves known. Still, he helped Bryson stand before going to work on pulling the glass shards from his side.

Bryson took King's arm and steered him back toward his bedroom. Glass cut into King's feet. He glanced down. Bryson was barefoot.

King stopped. "Wait." He lifted Bryson from the floor.

"What are you doing? You're hurt."

"Hush." King wasn't technically on the clock. He would backtalk if he wanted. Plus, everything hurt, and he was likely about to be tossed in the street anyhow once the shock wore off and Bryson truly realized how King was dressed. Then Archer would kill him because he knew too much. It truly had been a day.

Bryson let King carry him across the glass and into his bedroom. He shouldn't have, but King obviously wasn't in the mood to hear arguments. Bryson couldn't stop staring at King, watching for every twinge of discomfort. He had saved Bryson. More than that, Bryson didn't have as much as a scratch while blood poured from King's side. None of that took away from his beauty. His gorgeous whiskey eyes were meant to be lined in dark liner the way they were. The corset he had bought was ruined now, but it looked every bit as amazing as Bryson hoped.

Once inside King's bedroom, King set Bryson on the bed and went down on one knee. He checked the bottoms of Bryson's feet for glass and cuts.

"There's one small cut. Otherwise, I think you got off lucky."

"It wasn't luck."

King stood. He didn't meet Bryson's stare. "I understand if you feel you need to toss me out now, but I wish you wouldn't. Archer can't let me live if you do."

With the adrenaline wearing off, Bryson felt twice as emotional. King had saved him and seemed so calm and resigned. Bryson's chest hurt. He stared at the man who was used to being unwanted—who was used to being thrown away.

"Why would I toss you out?" Bryson didn't give him time to answer. "You should probably strip and let me dig out that glass. I might need to call someone to stitch you up."

Without a word, King tried reaching for the strings of the corset. He winced.

Bryson shot to his feet. "Let me." He moved to King's back and went to work on the string. To his shame, Bryson eyed King's wide shoulders and the way the corset accentuated his small waist and round ass. His mouth went dry. "I knew you'd look amazing in this. Tomorrow, I'll replace it."

King didn't say a word. He tried shrugging off the piece. King grunted and dropped his arms. It was obvious he couldn't get undressed alone.

Bryson circled him. His palms slid beneath the corset and pushed the material down King's arms. Without an ounce of shame, Bryson felt him up way more than necessary until he realized the clothing wouldn't move past King's waist. A large piece of glass had the material nailed to King's skin.

"Oh, shit." He ushered King to the bed. "Sit down. Let me see." It was deep. Blood poured from the wound. "I'll have to call someone. The glass might've punctured something, and you definitely need stitches."

"Just yank it out. I can stitch it."

Bryson's gaze shot to King's face. "Are you insane?"

King's jaw was set in a hard line. He motioned toward a nearby nightstand. "Grab a bottle from that drawer. I've got this."

Shock was the only reason he obeyed. Bryson yanked open the drawer and froze. There had to be fifty pill bottles inside. He went cold. They were all pain meds. His gaze moved King's way.

King's eyes were dead. "You may as well know all my secrets. Once the shock wears off, you'll put me out. Everyone does eventually."

Bryson closed the drawer. He spotted a pair of nearby house slippers. They were too big, but Bryson crammed his feet inside and headed back to the living room. It took a minute of searching through the debris, but he eventually found his phone. He dialed as he headed back toward King's room.

"Hello?"

"Dr. Young, this is Bryson Long. Are you free for a house call?"

Thankfully, the doctor didn't hesitate. "Of course. What's the problem?"

Honesty was best, and Andre Young was used to dealing with people like him. "Someone shot up my house and one of my guards was hit by flying glass. It looks pretty bad. At the very least, he needs stitches."

"I'm on my way. Be sure to leave the glass alone. If it hit anything vital, removing it could make things worse."

Bryson let himself inside King's room. King wore nothing but a red thong. He eyed King's body. There was a unicorn tattoo on his ass cheek. That caught Bryson's attention for a moment. Then, irritation ran down his spine. "Too late. It seems he ripped it out already." He honestly couldn't believe a genius like King would be so dumb. More likely, it was pure stubbornness.

A loud sigh came through the phone. "I'll hurry." The line disconnected.

It took Bryson a while to move the phone from his ear. King was a work of art. Bryson eyed every delectable inch until he realized the towel King held to his side was already soaked with blood.

King motioned toward a pair of pajama pants on the bed. "Will you help me?"

Bryson tossed his phone aside and rushed to help. He led King back to the bed. A trail of blood followed them. After a moment of panicked inspection, he realized the blood trail was from King's feet.

"Fuck." He dropped to his knees and inspected King's feet. They were ripped to shreds and still had glass buried in them. "You're such a stubborn ass." The words came out sounding enraged in Bryson's panic. "You carried me in here with no regard to yourself. What is wrong with you?"

A pained-sounding chuckle burst from King. “Would you like a list?”

Bryson shifted to his feet and headed into the bathroom. He soaked as many wash cloths as he could find in hot water before returning to King. Bryson found King trying to put on his pajama pants by himself while still holding the towel to his side.

“For fuck’s sake. Just stop. Let me take care of your feet first.”

“I don’t want to make you uncomfortable.”

Bryson’s eye twitched. “Sit down and be still.” Even Bryson heard the edge to his voice.

King did as told.

Bryson sat on the floor and went to work. He gently tugged slivers from King's feet, cleaning the blood as he went. King's gaze bored into the top of his head. It felt heavy, as if King touched him.

"Thank you for saving me."

"That's my job."

Bryson glanced up and met King's stare. "I'd say you went beyond your duty."

King didn't look away. "Maybe it's like you said. You're my friend."

They held each other's stare. Bryson had a million things he wanted to say. The bedroom door opened, stopping him from choosing a single one.

Andre stuck his head in the door. "I followed the trail of blood."

King dragged his pajama pants over his hips, obviously trying to hide the sexy underwear he wore.

Bryson glanced over his shoulder. “Give us two seconds.”

With a nod, Andre closed the door.

“That’s Dr. Young. Let’s get those pants on you.”

Relief etched King’s features. It was obvious he enjoyed dressing this way, but he was ashamed of it. Bryson wasn’t. He wanted more.

Chapter Three

By the time Bryson finished overseeing the cleanup and got someone to board up the house, pink streaks announced the coming sunrise. Bryson was mentally and physically exhausted. He had spoken briefly with Andre before he left, only long enough to find out King had lost a lot of blood and needed several stitches in various parts of his body. He had drugged King—like he couldn't have done that himself—and finished the stitches. Now, King rested quietly.

The whole night kept playing through Bryson's head. Everything from how beautiful King had looked to King saving his life and all the way around to King being an addict kept rolling through his brain. Oddly, he felt next to nothing when he thought about someone trying to kill him. He had no reason to be surprised. Threats had been slung his way for years. Not only that, but Bryson did business with crime lords. Getting shot at came part and parcel with that bullshit.

Once Bryson ensured the bodies on his lawn disappeared, he headed for King's bedroom. He poked his head in the door, fully expecting to find King asleep. Instead, he found King still dripping from the shower with a towel wrapped around his waist.

"Sorry. I should've knocked. I hoped you were resting."

King looked unfazed. "It's fine. I was covered in dry blood. It was starting to itch."

Bryson noticed King's bed was stripped. His bloody covers were on the floor. "Do you want me to send someone in here with fresh bedding?"

"Nah. It's morning now. I may as well stay up at this point."

For reasons he couldn't articulate, Bryson was disappointed. Maybe he had hoped to coddle King. He didn't know anymore. "Okay. I'll get someone to replace you for Monday, since you were screwed out of a night off. Plus, you're hurt. You need time to rest and heal. I'll reassess on Monday and decide how much longer you need to rest."

"I'm good. Don't worry about me."

King's nonchalance burrowed under Bryson's skin. "Fine."

At his curt tone, King cocked his head, as if trying to read Bryson's thoughts. He did his best to hide his overwhelmed emotions. "Did you get any sleep last night?"

Bryson shook his head.

King's shoulders rose and fell as he drew a deep breath and released it. He motioned for Bryson to come inside the room. Then he turned away and headed for the closet. As Bryson looked on, King dragged blankets from the closet and spread them across the bed. He pointed toward the bed as he moved to lock the door behind Bryson. "You. There."

Bryson hid a smile as he moved to do as told. On his side in bed, he watched King pull the blackout drapes and turn off the light. He resented the darkness when he heard King's towel hit the floor. The bed dipped beside him. Bryson measured each breath when his heart sped. He closed his eyes and tried to relax, but he knew King was only inches away. Bryson chewed his bottom lip. He fought the urge to roll and drape his leg across King's amazing body. Bryson wanted to set his head on King's chest and listen to his heart. He was forty-four. Until he met King, he hadn't realized how lonely he was or how empty his bed felt. But he didn't know how to close the gap between them, since this was so new to him.

He hadn't expected these feelings and desires.

Just when Bryson thought he might jump from the bed, King's heavy arm draped over him and hauled Bryson against his chest. King let out a content-sounding sigh. Bryson bit his lip to keep from smiling like an idiot. He was exactly where he wanted to be.

King hadn't been lying about being ready to face the day. He wasn't the least bit tired. He was used to going out late on Friday nights and staying gone the entire weekend. King partied at a club meant for people who matched him. It was the only time he felt free. But—somehow—here he was, holding Bryson. His body knew it was Bryson. Oddly, rather than being ready to fuck—as he would have expected—King just wanted to hold him and let him sleep.

Someone had tried to kill Bryson. That thought kept racing around his brain. Bryson wasn't taking the threats against him seriously enough. King didn't know how to force him to consider his safety first. The weekend guards should have left whoever shot up the place alive long enough to be questioned, and then put a bullet in their head. Now, they were no closer to ending this.

"Holy shit! Oh my God! Where is my dad? Was he hurt? Where is he?"

King bit back a groan at the sound of Kylian's shouts. Bryson never stirred. King quickly rolled from the bed and grabbed his still bloody pj pants, since they were the only thing he could find in the dark. He slipped into the hall before Kylian woke Bryson.

Kylian's blond hair was a mess. His blue eyes were wide with horror. They seemed to double in size when his gaze landed on King. "No. Is that Dad's blood?"

King made a calming gesture. "It's mine." King motioned toward his stitches. "Your dad is fine. He's sleeping."

Kylian's brow furrowed. He leaned to one side and eyed King's bedroom door. "With you? He's straight."

King wasn't surprised. "No. He stayed with me while I got stitched up and passed out before Dr. Young left."

Kylian's expression cleared. "Oh. Sorry. What happened here?"

As much as King didn't want to worry Kylian, someone needed to be concerned. "Someone shot up the house. One of the weekend guards killed whoever it was before anyone could be questioned."

"Are you okay?"

He had always liked Kylian. The kid was smart as hell and seemed genuinely kind. "I'm fine. Everyone is just a little exhausted."

Kylian chewed his bottom lip and stared at King's door. It was obvious he wanted to rush inside and check on his dad.

"If you want, I can wake him so you can check on him for yourself."

After a moment, Kylian's gaze slid his way. He looked young and vulnerable. Innocent. King had never been him. "No. I know you'll take care of him."

King dipped his chin. "If you plan to be around later, I can send him your way when he wakes up."

Kylian nodded. "Okay. I'll be around."

King nodded back and watched Kylian walk away before slipping back inside the room. He locked the door behind him. After stripping, King eased back into bed.

As King draped his arm over Bryson, Bryson spoke, surprising him. “Thank you for keeping him calm.”

“He’s a good kid.”

“I don’t know where he gets it from,” Bryson said, sounding thoughtful.

“I do.” King didn’t need to ponder that question. Bryson was a good man. At least, he was the best man King had ever met.

“About what Kylian said.”

“Go to sleep, Bryson.” Whatever Bryson had intended to say next; King didn’t want to hear it. For now, he had a small fantasy just for himself. One where Bryson fell in love with him—warts and all. They lived a normal life and King got to be happy and free. In the back of his mind, King knew it was only a dream that would never come true, but it was his. If Bryson confirmed he was indeed straight, that dream was dead, and it was all King had. He couldn't have it taken away. Not yet.

Chapter Four

It took longer than necessary for King to dress for work. Maybe he was getting old, but his stitches pained him more than he recalled. As a child, he had been tortured nonstop daily. He thought he was immune to pain, but it had been a long time since he needed stitches. King had gone years without getting his ass handed to him. He was out of practice. Life had gotten too soft. That didn't stop

King from wincing as he pulled his suit jacket on and buttoned it.

After some deep breathing, he slipped on his house shoes and hoped no one noticed. The cuts and stitches on his feet protested every step while barefoot. It was much worse with shoes squeezing his feet. Try as he might, he couldn't completely hide his limp as he made his way from his bedroom. When he reached the dining room, he was already sweating.

Kylian and Bryson looked up from their breakfast.

Bryson scowled. "I told you to take today off."

King poured himself some coffee. "To do what?"

Kylian stood and took away King's cup. He pointed at the table. "Sit. I swear. Men are so dumb and stubborn."

"You're a man," King pointed out as he claimed the chair on Bryson's other side.

With a wave of his hand, Kylian brushed away King's words. "Yeah, well. I'm gay, so it doesn't count."

"I'm gay too," King said, blowing a hole in Kylian's theory.

Kylian leveled his gaze upon King. "We are not the same kind of gay."

Honestly, King couldn't argue. Kylian was much softer than King had ever been allowed to be.

Obviously deciding his point had been made, Kylian finished making King's coffee and fixed King a plate. He didn't reclaim his seat until King had everything he needed.

"Thank you."

Kylian flashed him a sweet smile. "You saved my dad. It's the least I can do."

King didn't know how to respond. The subject made him uncomfortable.

Bryson took charge. "As to that, I'm still your boss. You're not working until you're healed. Those feet will never get better if you keep walking on them and tearing open your stitches."

King swallowed his irritation, but that didn't stop him from arguing. "I can't sit around and do nothing. This mystery person is getting bolder."

"You can and will," Bryson said, sounding as if the topic was closed.

King had to make him see reason. "Your son lives here. I need to know you're both safe." He swallowed his pride. "I care about you two."

Kylian touched his chest. "Awww. We care about you too. That's why you have to relax. I plan to go stay with my bestie for a while, so don't worry about me. Plus, college will start soon enough, and I'll be safely at Princeton."

King's gaze moved Bryson's way. He ate his breakfast as if nothing worried him. That irritated King more than he wanted to admit. Still, there might have been a bit of a growl to his voice. "What about you? How am I supposed to keep you safe?"

Bryson slathered jelly on his toast. He didn't look King's way. "You don't. We're going on a trip while you heal."

Confusion had King's brow furrowing. "Just because you're on vacation doesn't mean you're safe. Who are you taking with you?"

Bryson's laughing gaze swung King's way. He pointed his butter knife at King. "You and I are going on vacation. I knew your stubborn ass wouldn't stay in bed and I was right. So, vacation it is."

Kylian chimed in. "It'll be perfect. You know my best friend, Cheyenne, her family owns one of those cute little over-the-water bungalows in the Caribbean. They've said Dad can use it." Kylian made a dismissive gesture as if King argued. "Don't worry. They borrow Dad's cabin in Colorado for ski trips all the time. There's no way to connect Dad to the bungalow."

He had to admit it was a good plan, but he still didn't enjoy being put out to pasture. "I thought you wanted me to relax. Packing, getting to the airport, on a plane, even if it's a private one, and then getting to a bungalow where it'll be sandy doesn't sound like staying off my feet."

The twinkle that entered Bryson's eyes sent a chill down King's spine. "I'll pack for you. You can just sit on the bed, point, and I'll stick things in suitcases. As for everything else," Bryson motioned for someone to join them in the dining room, "we have this."

Horror washed over King as he turned his head. One of the weekend guards dragged a huge metal thing behind him by the handle like luggage. King already knew what it was before the guard handed Bryson the keys.

Bryson pressed a button on the keychain. "See. All you have to do is press the button, and it automatically unfolds."

It was an ECV scooter. King would rather die.

Bryson pressed the button again. "You just press the button again, and it folds into a lightweight piece that can be easily transported almost like oversized luggage. It'll be perfect."

King looked Bryson's way. "No."

Laughter flashed in Bryson's eyes. "We wouldn't be having this conversation if you had done what I asked and relaxed."

"I'll relax."

Bryson tsked. "Too late. You made your bed. Now you have to lie in it on an over-water bungalow." Bryson took another bite of his toast, looking triumphant. King wanted to die.

Holding true to his word, Bryson made King sit on the bed and tell him what to pack. He was more than a little excited at the idea of having King alone for a while. It felt like they were crawling closer to something unnamed. Bryson didn't know if he was ready for it or if everything was in his head. Maybe he shouldn't be excited at all. Things were a tad problematic for a thousand reasons. Bryson couldn't help what he felt, though, and he felt a lot.

When Bryson opened a dresser drawer, all thoughts of future issues disappeared. A rainbow of lace stared up at him. He felt King's eyes upon him. Bryson refused to let him be ashamed. He grabbed as much lace as possible and carried it to the open suitcase on the bed.

Bryson met King's stare as he dumped the pile in the suitcase. "When you're alone with me, I expect you to be comfortable and to be yourself."

King's expression gave nothing away.

Bryson went back to grabbing clothes. He looked for summer clothes and swim trunks. When he came across something sexy, he added it to the pile. He made sure to pick men's clothes too. Bryson wanted King to be comfortable, no matter the circumstances. What

Bryson wanted more than anything was for King to feel free with him.

King cleared his throat. “My makeup case is on the bathroom counter.”

Damn. He couldn’t wait to get to St. Lucia. Bryson dipped his chin and headed to the bathroom. It wasn’t hard to find the case. Unfortunately, it didn’t look like King had a huge variety. Bryson would fix that. He moved back to the bedroom and added the case to the suitcase.

“Kylian is lucky to have you. I bet growing up with you as a father was very freeing.”

The compliment moved Bryson, but it also hurt his chest. King sounded sad and resigned. He hadn’t known love. Bryson would change that. His insides froze at the thought. Had he fallen in love with King when he wasn’t looking? King was fucking amazing. He was a silent strength at Bryson's side. Bryson felt safe, even at the height of the worst attempts on his life, because he knew King wouldn't let anything happen to him. He had never had that. His marriage had been a nightmare. It occurred to Bryson that King deserved to know how special he was too.

A sad smile tugged at Bryson's lips. "That wasn't always true. I used to work all the time and barely saw him. Nothing mattered to me as much as making money." Bryson sat on the edge of the bed and held King's stare. "Obviously, I fell in love with my son the moment I knew he was on his way. Unfortunately, I thought the best way to show that love was to build something for his future, and I lost years with him I'll never get back. Then, I came back from a month-long business trip, and he was a shell of the child I'd left behind. He wouldn't speak to anyone. There was no happiness in him. My ex, Erica, she claimed he was just spoiled and angry because she wouldn't let him do whatever he wanted. Something about it didn't feel right, so I started asking questions on the sly. It was obvious none of the staff felt safe to talk to me. That had all my alarm bells clanging." Bryson took a breath. He hated reliving those days. "Finally, one of the newer chefs found me. It was obvious she was nervous, but determined. It turned out Erica was savagely abusive. She basically tortured Kylian anytime I wasn't looking. It turns out everyone was terrified of speaking up since Erica had threatened they would never work again if they said anything to me." He fought the urge to rub his chest. Bryson still wanted to find her and kill her. "I still don't know everything that happened to Kylian, but I divorced Erica. She lost all custody, and I put Kylian first. I still worked hard, but my work came second. Kylian went to therapy and slowly the smiles returned. I swore to myself he would always have what he needed most from me, and I know now that it wasn't money. He just needed me."

His gaze moved over King's face. He needed King to understand he was safe in this house. "He really cares about you. When he heard what you'd done for me, he gushed about how much he's always thought of you. You're not just some bodyguard who lives under my roof. If you don't know that, I'm sorry. I've proven many times over the years that I have no clue how to show people I care about them. But I do care about you," he added in case he hadn't made that clear.

King looked away. It was obvious Bryson had made him uncomfortable. "I care about you two too."

Bryson would take it. They were one step closer to each other. Before long, King would blink and wonder how he had become family. Bryson would settle for nothing less.

Chapter Five

For all of King's arguments, irritation, and humiliation, he felt more relaxed than he had in ages while kicked back in the bungalow. A private chef arrived with their dinner and Bryson still refused to let King leave the bed. The only bed in the bungalow. That detail hadn't escaped King. He didn't bring up the topic, though. Being with Bryson was too nice. Plus, truth be told, he had swallowed quite a few pills when they landed.

Bryson joined him on the bed. They sat side by side with their plates on a tray and stared out at the gorgeous blue and turquoise water.

"This place is amazing."

Bryson glanced his way. "Have you never been here? I would've thought Archer would've dragged you along at some point."

King's old boss, Archer, was a crime lord. They had traveled quite a bit, but it had never been leisure for him. "Archer used to be all over the place, but I didn't move in with him until after he married. His husband keeps him home these days. Now, before I went to work for Archer, I was freelance. I traveled a lot, but it was never for pleasure." He had to get in and out of every place he went quickly and quietly. That was one reason he had contracted with Archer. He had always been hunted. With Archer, he had gotten protection from law enforcement.

“Freelance?”

King ate a piece of shrimp before looking Bryson’s way. “You don’t want to know.”

“Of course, I do.”

He really didn’t. But if he ever wanted more with Bryson, King had to be honest. “I was raised for only one purpose.”

Bryson nodded. “So, you killed people?”

King looked away. He wasn’t proud of anything he had ever done. There was no way someone like Bryson could understand. It was incredibly possible to torture the humanity from someone, especially a child. King likely wasn’t sane.

King definitely couldn't handle being clean and sober. Some people's minds were just painful memories digging like worms twenty-four-seven until a person went mad. He felt Bryson's stare. King couldn't take it. Bryson was a good man. He would never understand.

King motioned toward the sofa. "Does that pull out into a bed?" He would take discomfort about their sleeping arrangement over discussing his past any day.

Silence met his question.

King looked Bryson's way. Bryson held his stare. He had no idea how long they sat like that in silence. King swore they kept getting closer, but he couldn't say which one of them moved. Then Bryson touched his lips to King's shoulder. He stayed there. King held his breath and waited.

When he didn't react, Bryson pulled away and went back to staring at the water. He looked embarrassed. "How's your side feeling?"

Something overcame King. They were alone, over two thousand miles from home. No one watched them. Before he had time to decide what he would do, King twisted. He snagged Bryson's throat and hauled him closer. His mouth covered Bryson's. He didn't know what to expect. Bryson surprised him by coming back at King every bit as hard. King bumped the tray of food between them with his knee. He quickly pulled away and set the food on the bedside table before going back for more. He didn't think. King didn't need reality any longer. He had the fantasy he had been clinging to for months.

In seconds, he had Bryson on his back. King's body covered his. Their kiss was unlike anything he had ever experienced. Probably because King hung out in seedy places, or maybe because he knew Bryson cared for him. Either way, King was in heaven. Bryson's kiss was sweet, hot, and did something to King's chest. Unlike other men, Bryson didn't tear at King's clothes. He wasn't demanding. King didn't feel pressured to move beyond savoring Bryson's mouth. That made things feel deeper than any kiss he'd had before now. This felt special.

Their kiss softened. Bryson's fingers found King's hair. Instead of pulling, the way King was accustomed, Bryson gently stroked, as if savoring him. The backs of

King's eyes burned. He felt how much Bryson cared.

King stroked Bryson's side, slowly making his way down Bryson's body. He buried his hand beneath Bryson's ass and squeezed. It felt every bit as good as he suspected. Bryson's erection couldn't be missed. King held Bryson's ass and ground down, causing friction between them. His mouth moved to Bryson's neck. He was too turned on to think clearly and knowing Bryson wanted him too made him half insane.

Bryson audibly gasped for air. "Can we slow down?"

King immediately rolled to the side, facing Bryson. He kept his leg over Bryson's legs and stroked his stomach. "Of course."

Bryson stared at the ceiling. His face was flushed. A happy-sounding laugh burst from Bryson before he turned his head and met King's stare. His eyes danced with happiness. "Sorry."

He was so sexy and King was too happy to care if they went any farther. "Why are you apologizing?"

"I've never been with another man."

That didn't surprise King.

Bryson's hands rose and fell in a helpless gesture. "I like you a lot and I want this. I'm just." He gestured again. "It's the logistics of it, I guess. Like I know I want you. I'm just not sure..."

He was so adorably embarrassed. King's heart went out to him. "It's okay. I'd never rush you or expect more from you than you're willing to do." He shrugged. "I like you a lot too. Being with you is enough for me. You can tell me when you're ready. If you never are, that's okay too. Your feelings matter to me."

Bryson looked so trusting. It tugged at King's heartstrings. "I'm ready. It's just that I don't know where to start."

King nodded and rolled from the bed. He held Bryson's stare and stripped. "Have you fantasized about me?"

This time, Bryson didn't blush. "Yes."

King gave him a sharp nod. Completely nude, he climbed onto the bed and settled on his back. "Whatever you did in your fantasies, do that."

"Are you sure?" Bryson sounded skeptical.

King met and held his stare. "There's nothing I won't do, especially for you."

Bryson moved to his knees and peeled off his shirt. King's gaze moved over his body. He had seen Bryson shirtless before, but it never got old. Bryson was furry. It was adorable. King couldn't help himself. He ran his finger down the line of hair that disappeared inside Bryson's jeans.

While King looked on, Bryson unbuttoned and unzipped his jeans. "I need your guidance. Don't go along with whatever to spare my feelings. I want to make you fly."

A smirk tugged at King's lips. "Don't worry. Don't overthink."

Bryson gave him a sharp nod. "I want to fuck you."

King was glad to hear it. He was too impatient to have to guide Bryson through his first time bottoming. King would have if that was what Bryson wanted, but King much preferred getting fucked. His cock throbbed. He especially preferred getting bent over with his skirt flipped up and his face buried. King loved it when he didn't have to think about how his face looked or if he was pleasing anyone. He enjoyed being free in one area of his life, taking his pleasure with no judgment.

"You'll need condoms and lube."

Bryson looked uncomfortable. "I have condoms, but I don't have lube."

King tried to keep him calm and in the moment. "Don't worry. Strip. I've got this."

King rolled from the bed. He dug through his bag and found his toiletries bag. It turned out he had condoms too, so they were good. He turned back and found Bryson nude and sitting on the edge of the bed. His gaze followed King.

“There are security monitors in my bedroom.”

King didn’t know how to respond to that announcement. It seemed like such an odd thing to say. He had never been inside Bryson’s bedroom. Bryson could have a dungeon in there for all King knew. “Okay.”

Bryson stroked his cock, making it harder for King to breathe. He really wanted this. Bryson held his stare, obviously unashamed of his desire. “I watch when you leave on the weekends.”

It hit King. Bryson had always known about his preference for women's clothing. He'd thought he had been so sneaky, making it out of Bryson's home without getting caught every Friday night. But Bryson had known all along and he had kept King's secret. Not only that, but the knowledge obviously aroused him.

"You didn't say anything."

"I am now."

King shifted from foot to foot, awkwardly holding condoms and lube. He didn't know what to say.

Thankfully, Bryson didn't seem to expect him to explain. "The first time I saw, I was shocked, but I couldn't stop rewinding the footage and watching you. Truth be told, even before I knew or you moved in with me, I couldn't stop watching you. You fascinate me."

"I'm a pill-popping head case."

Bryson shook his head. "You're beautiful and kind. My son loves you and I can't stop thinking about you."

King had honestly expected the night to be about sex. He had always known better than to expect more. Bryson was dangerous. He made King believe he could have everything. "There's no way you can know how terrifying you are to me."

Bryson's brow furrowed. His open confusion proved King's point. He could hurt King like no one else had in decades.

King crossed the room. He tossed the lube and condoms on the bed before moving to stand over Bryson. Bryson tilted his chin up to hold King's stare. King wouldn't leave him in the dark. Bryson needed to know how he could break King. King barely had a sliver of sanity left.

"No one has ever cared about me. Not my parents. No one. I can't even begin to imagine how bad it'll hurt when you no longer look at me the way you are now."

Bryson's hands slid up the back of King's thighs until he squeezed King's ass. He drew King closer. While holding King's stare, he leaned in and kissed King's stomach. "Or you could just trust me." He punctuated his words by licking King's crown.

King snapped. He toppled Bryson onto his back and straddled his body. Their mouths met and clashed, biting and sucking. They were carnal. Pure lust. All the months he had silently craved Bryson rose to the surface. King didn't care about foreplay. He would make it up to Bryson later. They had as much time as Bryson gave him. King would savor every second. Bryson didn't say anything else about slowing down. In fact, when King grabbed the lube, Bryson ripped into a condom. They both did their part to ready themselves. It was a frenzied mess that didn't calm until Bryson's cock pressed against the ring of muscles surrounding King's asshole. They held each other's stare. King pressed down, taking the dick he wanted. A stuttered-sounding gasp escaped Bryson.

King held Bryson's stare as he raised and lowered himself on Bryson's erection. He didn't know what he sought in Bryson's expression. Maybe he wanted to know if Bryson would backpedal and panic now that things were very real. He didn't.

Bryson touched King every place he could reach. "Damn. You're beautiful."

King felt beautiful on Bryson's dick. It was oddly empowering, knowing he was the only man Bryson had ever wanted. He had never truly felt special before now. Bryson couldn't know how much he meant or how much he had given King. He couldn't know how devoted and obsessed King was, all because Bryson wanted him when no one else ever had. Bryson treated him like he planned to keep him, as if—for once—he wasn't a stray to drop at the pound when his purpose was complete. King felt everything. Bryson's fingers wrapped around King's dick and he didn't think anymore.

King rode Bryson's palm and cock. He tilted his chin up and sucked air as he struggled closer to orgasm. "Fuck. You have no idea how many times I've pictured being on your dick like this."

Bryson groaned. "Don't talk like that. I've wanted you for too long. I'm already fighting not to come before you."

King dropped his chin and held Bryson's gaze. "Do it. I want to watch you come unglued. I want to fantasize there's nothing between us as you come. Pump my ass full of cum. I want to picture your cum dripping from my ass."

Bryson pumped King's dick faster, as if he would be the one to spit cum from King's cock. A cry tore from his lips. He kept pumping until that same shout escaped King. Cum covered Bryson's stomach and chest. King watched it happen. It was like he marked his territory. Then he squished the mess between them as he claimed Bryson's mouth. He wanted to taste Bryson's satisfaction. As his body let go of its final spasm, the worst thought hit. What if this was it? What if this one experiment with King was enough for Bryson? Maybe that was all this was—a walk on the other side, and now that Bryson had his fun, it wouldn't happen again. Fear choked him.

Bryson stroked his face. "You should rest. Next time, I'll be braver."

Like that, the air cleared. King could breathe again. It was Bryson. Bryson would never hurt him.

Bryson couldn't stop touching King. He was tired, but then again, he wasn't. His body hummed and his mind raced. But there was also a peace in Bryson's heart, and he didn't want to miss a single thing. He kept going over every second of their lovemaking. While he had panicked a bit at first, his desire had won in the end. Now Bryson wanted to try everything. He wanted to hear King confess he had fantasized about Bryson again.

"Were you serious earlier when you said you'd pictured yourself with me before? I know people say things in the heat of the moment." Damn. He sounded like an insecure teen. The feeling doubled when King didn't respond right away.

He covered Bryson's hand on his chest with his and stroked Bryson's knuckles. "You were wearing work boots the first time I saw you. I remember because it struck me as odd that this billionaire who should be out playing golf was dressed to work."

A smile tugged at Bryson's lips. "I've done every job in my business. I'm not scared to work."

King kissed his forehead. "I know that now, but I didn't then. It was just odd to me because I'd never met a man like you. That was the first detail about you that caught my attention. Then I noticed the way you actively listened to everyone, like you weren't better than them and their opinions mattered. One day, you were bent over plans with Archer, and I just stared at you. I remember wishing you would lift your head and see me the way I saw you. Then, you did, and—for a moment—I couldn't breathe. I don't know why you looked at me. You were still speaking on the topic at hand, planning out land plots for Archer's warehouses. But it was like you involved me in the conversation and sought my opinion, even though I didn't have one. I don't know. You just crawled into my head and under my skin. I can't stop wanting you."

"You had a hickey that day." Bryson knew exactly the moment King spoke about. "Your collar almost hid it, but I always notice every detail about you. I kept trying to make it through my meeting with Archer, but I couldn't stop looking your way. That fucking hickey. It bothered me and I didn't understand why." Bryson paused and thought better of his words.

"That's not true. I seethed with jealousy, and it made no sense. Not one time in my life had I wanted another man, but the thought of someone else marking your skin filled me with rage. Some part of me thought, if I hold his stare, he'll finally see that I'm the one who wants him. No one else should touch him but me. I know it was insane."

"Huh."

Bryson moved up onto his elbow so he could see King's face. "What was that 'huh' about?"

"That wasn't a hickey. I'd gotten into a fight the night before. But you had a hickey two weeks later, and I wanted to strangle you."

A smile exploded across Bryson's face. "That wasn't a hickey. Kylian came home covered in cat hair, which fired up my allergies. I was covered in hives and trying to tear my skin off from the itching."

The huge smile King wore was everything. Bryson wanted to keep him like that, but he also wanted to know every detail of King's life. "Why were you in a fight?"

King shrugged. "When you're like me, even when you're in supposed safe spaces, there's still the occasional asshole who thinks they can hurl slurs at my clothing choices. I had to remind someone a skirt didn't mean I couldn't kick their ass."

An image of King in that corset and skirt flashed through Bryson's mind. "Show me."

King's brow furrowed. "You want me to kick your ass?"

A laugh burst from Bryson. "I want you to put on a skirt."

"Oh." King looked thoughtful for a moment. "I don't think I have one here."

A slow smile spread across Bryson's lips. "I threw in a black leather one while grabbing some other things."

King's gaze moved over Bryson's face, as if searching for something. "You honestly like that side of me."

It wasn't a question, but Bryson still treated it as one. "I do. Not only are you incredibly gorgeous, but you're authentically you when you dress how you want."

King moved as if to stand. "If that's really what you want."

Bryson set his hand on King's chest. "Wait. I brought you here to rest. Let me grab it. I've let you stand too much today already. Plus, I know which suitcase it's in." He felt King relax. Bryson climbed over him and padded to the suitcase, uncaring of his nudity. In fact, he enjoyed giving King a show. He easily found the leather piece and carried it back to bed. Bryson stood at the edge of the bed while King shimmied on the skirt. He moved to his knees and zipped it.

Bryson's dick hardened. He watched the way King's muscles moved and how the skirt fell against his skin, barely hiding his cock. Bryson needed more. He moved back to the suitcase and found a hot pink thong.

"This too."

Heat flashed in King's eyes as he went through the motions of struggling into the underwear without leaving the bed. He shifted back to his knees when they were halfway up his thighs so he could tug them into place. After adjusting his junk, King let the skirt fall back in place.

Bryson stroked his throbbing cock. "Show me."

King didn't pretend he didn't understand. He turned and went face down, ass up, and flipped the skirt up so Bryson could see the way the underwear disappeared inside his crack. His ass was so goddamn sexy with that hot pink string. All Bryson could think about was fucking him just like that. He grabbed another condom from the dresser and ripped into it.

"Don't move."

King didn't budge.

Bryson rolled the condom down his length. Then he found the lube before crawling onto the bed and moving to position himself behind King. He pushed the string aside and eyed King's waiting hole. The muscles in his stomach clenched. He had already had King once. All the sex in the world with King would never be enough. He lubed his fingers and wet King's hole.

"You have to push some inside too."

Bryson quietly followed King's directions. He poked his lubed finger inside King's asshole.

King moaned.

Bryson thought about some things he had done to himself in the dark. He stuck a second lubed finger inside and searched for King's prostate. He knew when he had found it. King made a sound that made Bryson's cock jump in jealousy. He wanted to rub that spot with his dick and force King to make that sound again. With one hand, he kept the panties held to the side while he led his erection to King's waiting hole. As it had last time, it surprised him how much pressure it took to get inside. Then King's body greedily accepted him. He almost had to fight against the pull.

Bryson tried several angles before King made a sound that nearly forced an orgasm from him. Bryson held that position and thrust. King's knuckles whitened where he held the sheets. A loud moan echoed through the room. Bryson did it again. His eyes fought to close against the pleasure. He kept them open. Bryson didn't want to miss a thing. Each thrust happened a little faster than the last. Bryson didn't want to finish before King again, but he didn't see how King could come like this. He couldn't stop, though. King's hole felt too good. He was locked in ecstasy. Bryson was too far gone to stop. His sanity would snap if he didn't get to shoot his load inside this perfect ass. King was right. That was a hot-ass fantasy. He wanted to sit between King's cheeks and watch his cum as it leaked from that gorgeous rosebud. Bryson wanted all the secret longings he experienced since meeting King to come true.

Bryson craved knowing what it was like to have King's heavy cock on his tongue. He wanted to lick King's balls and spend hours making him beg. Bryson could spend the rest of his life between these cheeks. A gasp ripped from King and rent the air. King's asshole tried sucking him deeper. Bryson froze while buried to the hilt. He squeezed his eyes shut and lived in the moment, experiencing everything as King's body milked him. He moaned as the pressure climbing his shaft turned into waves of pleasure. His hips automatically rolled, riding each jet that spat from his dick. Once again, he dreamed his juices filled King. One of these days, King would marry him, and he would get to make the fantasy real. He forced his eyes open so he could stare at the man on his cock. It wasn't the first time Bryson had told himself he would marry King, and he always got his way.

Chapter Six

THEY SPENT THREE WEEKS sequestered in the bungalow of freedom. That was how King liked to think of it. He had worn different outfits and Bryson had ordered more for him to be waiting when they got home. King had shown Bryson a dozen ways to please him and watched Bryson blow a dozen more. He honestly didn't want to go home, where he knew he would have to go back to being the guard. Bryson wouldn't freely touch him anymore. King would sit on the sidelines and melt into the background. Bryson would go back to being the amazing father and businessman. King would be nothing again.

In the tiniest corner of his mind, King clung to a ridiculous dream. One where they got home, and Bryson stayed exactly as he had been the past three weeks. That was pure fantasy, of course. He had always known he would never have that life. Still, he was allowed to dream. No one had stolen that from him, and Bryson had belonged to him for a moment. That was something no one could take from him.

They made it home by five pm and Bryson headed straight for his office. King stayed on his heels, as always.

"I just need to catch up on my emails."

"Of course."

Bryson flashed him a smile. He brushed the back of his knuckles against King's as they stepped through the door of his office. King drew a steadying breath as Bryson made his way behind his desk. That touch meant something. Maybe not that Bryson would openly claim them, but at the very least, they weren't done.

"Dad!" Kylian burst into the office before Bryson was fully seated. "I heard you were back."

"Hey, baby. I didn't think you'd be home."

Kylian circled the desk to hug Bryson. "I missed you." His gaze moved between them. "Why are two still so pale? Did you go outside at all?"

King could practically feel Bryson trying not to look his way. Instead, Bryson smiled, keeping his expression innocent. "Some of us believe in sunscreen and don't brown as lovely as you do."

Kylian rolled his eyes. "Please don't lecture me about sunscreen again."

"I'm just saying you'll wish you'd worn it when you get to be my age."

An adorable-sounding snort burst from Kylian. "Anyway, I only came home to grab some stuff. I'm headed back to Cheyenne's so we can finish making a list of everything we need for our graduation trip."

Bryson nodded. "Okay. Take a guard with you."

Kylian headed for the door. “I always do. Love you guys.” He didn’t wait for a response before slipping away.

They exchanged a glance and a smile. Bryson shook his head. King was certain they shared the same thought. It must be nice to be young.

Sean strolled in before either of them could say a word. The lanky red-haired guard stayed completely professional, as always. “Welcome back, Mr. Long. Everything was quiet while you were away and all the repairs from our little incident have been completed.” His light green gaze swung King’s way. “You received several packages a few days ago. They were left outside your bedroom door.”

“Thank you.” Again, King fought the urge to look Bryson’s way.

Bryson left him no choice. “You should unpack, King. No doubt you have things to catch up on too. I’ll let you know if I need anything.”

King dipped his chin. It was hard, but he did his best not to give them away. He didn’t have time to say a word. He got rushed through the door by Sean’s exit.

Sean’s professionalism broke the second they were alone and headed in the same direction. “How was the trip? I’ve heard it’s beautiful there.”

“It was nice, and the island is beautiful.”

Sean either didn’t hear or chose not to hear the disinterest in King’s voice. “I wish I’d get picked for tropical vacations.

Not that you didn't deserve it after the badass way you saved Mr. Long, but that's never the jobs I get. I usually get stuck going to Cheyenne's house with Kylian. Then I have to listen to them talk about hot guys while they experiment with various makeup tutorials with me as their canvas."

That surprised King. He looked Sean's way with a smile. "That honestly sounds fun. At least they're including you. You could get left standing in the corner, completely ignored while suffering a migraine from the chatter."

Sean shrugged. "That's true. I did find out I look pretty fucking amazing in eyeliner and at least there's always wine."

King snorted and shook his head.

Apparently, that was all Sean needed to keep going. "I know. Kids these days, right? When I was nineteen, I would've been ripped a second asshole if I went out drinking with friends. But Kylian's a good kid. He honestly never does anything wrong."

King nodded. Kylian was a good kid.

Sean headed toward the front door as they reached the living room. "It was good chatting with you. I have to get back to patrol."

"Have fun with that."

Sean's chuckle followed him out the door. King headed for his bedroom. Sean hadn't been exaggerating. Several packages were stacked outside his door, along with his luggage. He was positive there were way more than he had seen Bryson order. King unlocked his room and carried everything inside. It took a few trips.

He unpacked first, separating his dirty clothes into piles. The men's clothing, he sent down the laundry chute. The women's clothes, he tossed into a laundry basket to hand wash later. With everything put away, he took a long, hot shower before wrapping a towel around his waist and settling into open boxes.

The first few were all lingerie and outfits he recognized from their online shopping spree. Then he came to a package with three different corsets. They were all various colors and designs. Each one looked handmade and extremely expensive. King eyed each one with his heart in his throat. Bryson was amazing. Next was a new makeup kit filled with high-end name brands. King wondered if he might cry. It was too much, and he still had packages to go. There were two pairs of sexy shoes. He left the smallest box for last. When King opened it, his breath caught before he even saw what was inside. It was a small blue box from Tiffany's. Inside, he found a gold necklace with a Lynn Pendant. Four diamonds with a golden X separating them. He couldn't look away.

A brisk knock landed on the door before Bryson strolled in. His expression fell when saw King holding the necklace. "Oh no. I didn't get to see your face when you opened that. I tried to hurry."

King blinked, trying to keep his emotions under control. "You're seeing it now." His voice sounded hoarse. "I just opened it."

A bright smile lit Bryson's face. "Good. Let's get it on you, then." He crossed the room and took the necklace from King. He placed it around King's neck while King sat stunned into silence. Bryson backed up and stared at his handiwork. "Beautiful."

In that moment, King wished for bravery. He wanted to beg Bryson to tell him where they stood or where this was headed. King needed to know he was more than Bryson's bodyguard. But King was scared as hell he wouldn't like the answer and he needed to hang on to this as long as possible. He swore to himself he wouldn't be bitter when Bryson stopped focusing on him. Even when whatever this was, was done, King would protect Bryson until his last breath. He loved

Bryson. It mattered not at all to his heart that Bryson would never love him back.

Bryson wanted to take a picture of the way King stared at him. He wanted to be able to take it out of his pocket any time he wished and remember this moment. King looked at him like he loved him. No one other than his son had loved him in a long time. Bryson wanted to shower King in extravagant gifts and keep King looking at him just like he did in that moment because he didn't for one moment think it had anything to do with the gifts.

King snagged the tail of Bryson's t-shirt and lured him closer. He stood between

King's knees and wound his arms around King's neck. King stared up at him. "Why did you do all of this?"

"Because you deserve it," Bryson answered honestly. A smile tugged at his lips. "And I want to see you draped in things as gorgeous as you."

King's hands moved to the button on Bryson's jeans. He popped it loose. King held Bryson's stare as he slowly slid Bryson's zipper down. "I worried you wouldn't want me anymore once we got home."

That shook Bryson. "Why would you think that? I thought you understood you're the only person I want."

King set Bryson's cock free. "I get inside my head sometimes. It's kind of ugly in there. I'm the one thing I can't escape from my past." Before Bryson could respond, King dipped his head and sucked Bryson's dick into his mouth.

Bryson lost all rational thought. All he could do was watch while King got him hot. It was impossible to think clearly with King's talented mouth latched onto his cock. He knew he should pull away and make King talk to him, but he couldn't. King had already won this round. Instead, he stroked King's hair and rode his tongue. He savored every second. One of these days, King would understand he was it for Bryson. Until then, he would be present and shower King with gifts. He didn't know how else to show his love. There was no way he could fix King. Still, Bryson hoped he healed him some with a soft touch.

Greedy suction on his dick pulled him from every ounce of worry. He took what King gave. As always, with King's full focus on him, Bryson didn't last long. Way before he was ready, each breath came out sounding like a moan. He openly fucked King's mouth, taking what he wanted, abusing King's throat. Desperation had him rocking into every downward bob. He held King's hair in a death grip. His toes curled, trying to get better traction. When his orgasm hit, Bryson had to lock his knees to keep from going down. All he knew was ecstasy. He lost all grip on reality.

In a flash, he was beneath King. King's towel had disappeared. His mouth covered Bryson's. Bryson tasted his cum on King's tongue. He would spend every night of the rest of his life just like this if it was the last thing he did. King had nothing to worry about. Bryson would love him forever.

Chapter Seven

Six months later...

As much as Kylian would like to say he was having the time of his life in college, just living it up and partying with all his new friends, that wasn't at all how things had gone. None of his high school friends had made it into Princeton. He had started from the bottom with no friends. Since his dad—thankfully—bought him a house to live in off campus, he didn't even have a dorm room buddy. That was probably a good thing, since everyone hated the new gay boy in town. Having zero friends made it easier for him to stay focused on his studies. Not that he had any clue what he wanted to do with his life. In high school, he had only wanted to do his best, get into the best college, and make his dad proud. He hadn't thought past that. Now he only felt lost.

Truthfully, as much as Kylian couldn't wait to get home for Christmas break to people who liked him, Kylian also dreaded it. Even though he knew it didn't make sense, he felt like he was going home as a failure.

While in a dark place, he moved his flight time to later in the night. Then he had a brighter moment and left for the airport seven hours early, hoping to change the time back. If he couldn't, then he would be there already and would have to get on the plane tonight.

With his head down and his suitcase in tow, Kylian headed toward his car. Honestly, he could just make the five-hour drive home, but then he would have to make the drive back, and he wanted to stay as long as possible. As he pulled his keys from his pocket, a hand covered his mouth, and his feet left the ground. He didn't hesitate. Kylian immediately fought for his life. He sank his teeth into the palm across his mouth hard enough to draw blood. A shout cried out behind him. Kylian kicked, determined to survive, landing solid heels to the man's shins. He dropped his chin and then threw his head back, cracking his attacker across the nose, pulling out every trick King had shown him. Then he went limp, throwing his weight forward and catching his attacker off guard.

"Goddamn it."

Kylian hit the ground when his efforts finally freed him. He didn't waste time. Kylian took off running. He didn't make it far. An arm snatched his waist hard enough to knock the wind from his lungs and a prick stung his neck. The world went fuzzy and then dark. The ground tilted beneath him as everything disappeared.

To him, it seemed like only moments passed. He came awake with a start. His heart raced into his throat as soon as his eyes opened. He was in the back of a moving vehicle. It was obviously a larger SUV. He could see the streetlights passing overhead through the large back window. Duct tape covered his mouth and wrapped his hands and feet so tightly, he couldn't feel them any longer. His mind raced. He didn't know what to do next. They had obviously drugged him. He didn't know how long he had been out or how far they had gone. His brain was still too fuzzy to think clearly. He needed to make a plan.

The car slowed and turned. He still hadn't figured out what to do next before the car stopped. Kylian braced himself. He didn't know how he would fight at this point, but he would try. The back opened, and a pissed off looking muscle-bound guy stared down at Kylian with hatred bleeding from two black eyes. Dried blood covered his face. It looked as if his nose was broken. The part of Kylian that wasn't scared he was about to die, which wasn't much, wanted to pat himself on back. At least he hadn't died without leaving a mark.

The musclehead easily plucked Kylian from the back and tossed him over his shoulder. The air left Kylian's lungs in a painful whoosh. Every step the guy took jammed the guy's shoulder into Kylian's sternum, stealing his breath until Kylian thought he might faint. Then he was dumped unceremoniously on a hardwood floor. It wasn't easy, but he pushed himself to his knees. He would fight until his dying breath.

A man sat on a leather chair. Kylian had been surrounded by money his entire life. This man bled wealth from his haircut to his thousand-dollar pants. His eyes were the clearest green Kylian had ever seen. His dark hair was perfectly styled.

His gaze moved from Kylian to the man who had kidnapped him.

He opened his mouth and the thickest Irish accent Kylian had ever heard poured out. “Don’t tell me this tiny sprite did that to your face.”

The man didn’t respond.

Kylian didn’t look his attacker’s way. It was obvious whoever this guy was, he was in charge.

A smirk pulled at the man’s lips. “Oh, my. He has spunk. Remove the tape.”

A sharp knife appeared in front of Kylian. He tried hard not to panic. Even once the tape was sliced away from his hands and feet, Kylian didn’t react. He needed to regain feeling in both before he struck. Kylian needed to be at his best. He also didn't want that knife to end up cutting his throat. The tape ripped from his lips, taking a layer of skin with it. He refused to react. Kylian wouldn't give anyone the pleasure of seeing his pain.

"Who are you?" It probably didn't matter. If he was dead, the information would die with him.

The smirk grew. "My name means nothing to you, but it also doesn't matter if you have it. I'm Rian McKinley and you are the delectable Kylian Long."

"Damn. A full government name. I'm really not leaving here alive."

One dark eyebrow rose at Kylian's comment. "On the contrary. I have a job for you. You see, your father is starting trouble he can't handle. New York belongs to me. It belongs to my family.

There won't be any building of warehouses for Archer Woods in my territory. No weapons, drugs, or stolen goods go through New York without my say so."

Kylian had no clue what Rian meant. "My dad is just a land developer. If you have a problem with this Archer guy, you should take it up with him."

Rian's cold gaze moved over Kylian's face. "That's a shame. You're on the edge of getting killed over something you know nothing about. As to taking things up with Archer, don't worry your pretty self about that one. For now, it's fun for me to torment Archer from afar. To make him wonder why he can't keep anyone working on his little project. And unfortunately, at the moment, Archer is out of my reach. But you, you're not." Rian stood and crossed the room. He came to stand over Kylian. His fingers brushed down Kylian's jaw. To his shame, Kylian didn't move away. He was too mesmerized—like waiting for a cobra to strike. "You're very much within my reach."

A chill ran down his spine.

Rian's light green eyes stayed locked on Kylian. Kylian couldn't decipher his expression. If he wasn't a sane man, he would swear it was lust in Rian's eyes. Surely not. The man had him tied and had threatened his life.

"Warden is about to take you home. You'll be blindfolded, but unharmed." Rian bent and went eye to eye with Kylian. "Then you'll go home to daddy and take him a message. If he doesn't stop his bullshit, his precious baby boy will never be seen again. Look into my eyes,

Kylian. Tell me I won't kill you. Make sure he knows it."

There was no way in hell Kylian would be doing that. As far as he was concerned, this never happened. His father had done everything for him. Saved him. He had given up so much to keep Kylian safe and give him the best life. Kylian wouldn't worry him like this. Rian could come for him if he wanted. Kylian would be ready for him next time.

Each day, King fell a little more in love with Bryson. Every day, it got a little harder. He stood or sat in the same places he had always stood or sat while Bryson lived his life. If they were alone, they would speak freely or lock themselves in Bryson's office for a quick tryst. Bryson came to him every night. Sometimes they just held each other until Bryson sneaked away. Every day, King was a little more confused and a lot more bitter. He didn't understand why they were hiding unless Bryson was ashamed.

That thought scratched at the back of King's brain while he silently watched Bryson holding an online meeting. Six months. For six months, he had done this. He had thought maybe when Kylian left for Princeton, things would change, but no. Now Christmas was a week away. The idea that he might have to sit on the edge of the room while Kylian and Bryson played family together without him on Christmas morning was mentally torturing him.

King watched the way Bryson's lips moved. His hands. There was so much love inside King, he thought he might explode. He kept wondering why he did this. Then Bryson's gaze slid his way. King's breath caught. The love. That was why. He adored every inch of Bryson. King had never felt this way about anyone. Bryson ended his meeting and King couldn't wait for his attention about anything at all, even if it was only Bryson sending him on an errand.

"What time do you suppose Kylian will be here? I honestly thought he would be here last night."

King knew nothing about college life, but he adored that Bryson sought his opinion. "He probably wanted to go out with friends before leaving them for a few weeks. You know Kylian. He's a social butterfly. Have you tried texting him?"

Bryson pulled out a sheepish smile. "I don't want to be overbearing. He's an adult now."

"Would you like me to text him? I'm not above being overbearing."

Bryson's smile grew. "No. It's okay. I'll give him until tonight and then I'll panic. Plus, I have something else I need you to do."

"Anything." King didn't hesitate. There was nothing he wouldn't do for Bryson.

A wicked glint flashed in Bryson's eyes, making King's mouth go dry. "You still haven't worn that pink sweater for me. Go put it on and wait for me."

King dipped his chin and stood. He didn't need to be told twice. King headed to his room without looking back. In fact, he couldn't get there quickly enough. The thought of having Bryson alone was enough to light a fire beneath his feet.

Inside his room, King stripped and found the fuzzy sweater. He spent a moment trying to decide what to wear with it when a wicked smile stretched his lips. He pulled on the sweater and settled on the bed. With the pillows stacked behind him, he waited bare-assed for Bryson to join him. The moment his bedroom door opened, and Bryson's heated gaze landed on him, King's cock grew.

"Damn." Bryson closed the door behind him and locked it. "Look at you, looking like a goddamn feast." Bryson peeled off his shirt. "Good thing that's exactly what I had in mind." He finished stripping and climbed onto the mattress. His gaze ate King alive. King felt sexy beneath Bryson's stare. Sometimes, from nowhere, it struck him how beautiful his life was now. All because Bryson existed. The bitterness melted away, the way it always did beneath Bryson's stare.

Bryson kissed King's inner thigh. He stared up the line of King's body as his lips moved higher. Each breath King took came harder and faster than the last. He ached to feel Bryson's hot mouth surrounding his dick. But King knew Bryson never really did that since he didn't feel confident in his abilities. Bryson touched his lips to King's cock.

King held his breath. His eyes burned from his refusal to blink.

Tentatively, Bryson opened his mouth over the tip of King's dick and sucked.

A moan came from King's soul. He gripped the covers beneath him. The last thing he wanted was for Bryson to stop because King got too aggressive. He also knew this could end any second.

Bryson turned bolder by the second until he bobbed on King's cock, obviously getting into blowing King. When he abruptly pulled away, King fought a groan. He knew Bryson would pleasure him one way or another, but that mouth...

"It's okay."

Bryson smirked and found the lube. He didn't say anything at King's reassurance. His amused expression confused King until Bryson settled back down between King's thighs. This time with lubed fingers. He went back to sucking King. His wet fingers found King's asshole. He fingered King. Sounds of pleasure rumbled from King. His hips rocked. Then Bryson's fingers found King's prostate as he sucked hard. King buried his fingers in Bryson's hair. It was out of his control.

"Oh, god, Bryson. Just like that. Everything about you drives me wild. You're perfect." He panted, trying to cling to his sanity. "I'm going to come. You feel too good. Stop now if you don't want that. I can't—" A cry ripped from King's throat as he unexpectedly blew. He shook as cum filled Bryson's mouth and ran down

King's length, soaking his balls. Before he had time to recover, Bryson shot upward and impaled King.

He froze. Horror etched his features as he stared down at King. "Fuck. I forgot the condom."

They stared at each other.

King was the first to break. He lured Bryson's close so he could steal a kiss. King needed to feel his feelings before he confessed his heart. He swiped his lips across Bryson's. "It's okay. Before you, I hadn't been with anyone else in over ten years."

Bryson pulled away enough to hold King's stare. He looked shocked. "It was seven for me. I just..." Bryson took a shaky breath. "Nothing felt right anymore. I was missing something. I hadn't met you."

For much longer than necessary, they held each other's stare. Then Bryson's hips rocked forward, and King didn't stop him. Their lips met. They shared each other's air. King's heart swelled until he thought he might burst. He wondered for a moment if he would cry. Everything about them was perfect and was everything he begged the universe for when he was alone at night. They felt permanent in a way they hadn't before. He had hope. Now, he needed Bryson to leave him leaking.

Hours passed. Bryson couldn't stop touching King or trying to make him moan. He expected to be exhausted. Instead, Bryson was exhilarated. Bryson wanted to do more than make love to King. He wanted to *show* him love. Bryson bounced on his knees next to King's limp body. "I know. I know. Let's make hot chocolate. It's cold outside. It's almost Christmas. We should put on our warmest pjs, start a fire in the fireplace, and cuddle up with cocoa." Even Bryson heard the ridiculous happiness in his voice. He didn't care. Bryson was happy.

"Sounds great." King sounded as exhausted as he looked. But he still found the strength to topple Bryson onto his chest so he could claim Bryson's lips. A loud clap rent the air as King's hand landed solidly on Bryson's ass. He squeezed Bryson's ass cheek. "Let's go. I want this dream night you've painted."

With a chuckle, Bryson scrambled from the bed and threw on the bare minimum of clothes. "I'll meet you in the kitchen in ten."

King gave him a tired thumbs-up, pulling a laugh from Bryson. Bryson slipped from the room and raced to his bedroom. He needed to clean up a little and find some pajamas. The pure joy in Bryson's heart had Bryson practically dancing in place. He couldn't stop smiling. It felt like King and he were moving toward something amazing. He actually had a plan for them, but there were a few kinks to iron. First, and most importantly, he had to talk to Kylian. Bryson hadn't openly dated anyone in front of Kylian since his split from Kylian's mom. Kylian's safety and happiness had always come first to him. Second, there was the issue of King's position with him. While he didn't doubt King would always keep him safe, no matter what position he held in Bryson's life, Bryson couldn't have the other guards sniping at King. Plus, he didn't want King to still be considered an employee. He hadn't quite figured that one out yet. Bryson didn't want to hire a replacement. He abhorred when King was off duty and other people followed Bryson everywhere. It was uncomfortable. They would work it out, though. Somehow.

With clean skin and pajamas in place, Bryson practically skipped to the kitchen. He found King already there, wearing a teddy bear onesie and working on their hot chocolate. He already had a plate of sugar Christmas tree-shaped cookies set out on the island for them.

King turned when Bryson approached. The smile he wore was everything. King carried two cups to the island.

Bryson stole his chance. He wrapped his arms around King's waist and held tight. His lips found the spot between King's shoulder blades.

King twisted in his arms.

Bryson braced his palms on the island on either side of King. Words rose in his throat. It was well past the point he should have confessed his feelings. King's head slowly lowered. Bryson knew he should stop King and say the three words that lived on his tongue. The back door swung open, and Bryson jumped away. Even he wasn't sure why. It just happened.

Kylian stepped inside, dragging a suitcase behind him. He froze at the sight of them. His gaze moved slowly between them, as if assessing the situation. "Hey. Did I interrupt something?"

"Of course not. I'm so happy to see you."

Kylian still didn't budge at Bryson's reassurance. "What's going on here?"

Bryson laughed. "Nothing." He flashed a glance King's way, looking for reassurance. Instead, he saw hurt and betrayal in King's eyes.

Even still, King didn't expose him. King motioned toward the cups and cookies.

"Security saw you coming. We made hot chocolate for you, and I set out some cookies."

Bryson's throat swelled. While King did an okay job of hiding his hurt while talking to Kylian, Bryson saw the pain behind every word.

Kylian ditched his bag and skipped across the room. "Awww. Thank you, King. You're amazing. It's been the longest day, and this is perfect." He gave King and huge hug. Bryson watched them with his heart in his throat. Kylian kissed King's cheek. "I missed you. Are you joining us for cocoa and cookies?"

King's brittle smile stomped Bryson's windpipe. "No. You need some time with your dad. He's been missing you and bemoaning your absence every day. You two should catch up without me."

Bryson tried like hell to catch King's eye as Kylian moved to hug him, but King blatantly didn't look his way. While Kylian still held tight, King slipped away, and Bryson fought the urge to call his name. Right there, before his eyes, Bryson watched every beautiful dream he had created fall from his grasp. He had broken the man he loved.

To the bottom of his soul, King hurt. He had known. Deep down, there had never been any doubt. Bryson was ashamed of him. He didn't know if it was the dating a man aspect or that King was beneath him. Whatever the reason, King had felt it. He had known this night would come. At first, he had thought they were just playing it cool since he was Bryson's guard. Then time kept passing and King had stayed a secret. He had thought he loved Bryson enough to deal. Unfortunately, King had greatly underestimated how badly Bryson's open denial of them would hurt. He still saw Bryson laughing at the idea of anything going on between them.

King paced his bedroom. It was Friday night. He should go out. There were other places he could be. Places where he didn't feel unwanted. The house had gone quiet ten minutes ago. He could change and just go. King knew how to drown himself. He was damn near an expert at becoming someone else for two days a week just to survive. King could do it again. He rubbed his chest. Why did his life have to keep being like this? Other people got to be happy. Why not him? King didn't understand. He had thought things were perfect. Now he couldn't deal.

King didn't waste time. He didn't try to look hot. He grabbed the first sexy clothes he came across and pulled them on. It was too cold for a skirt. So he only had to find a pair of jeans and a sexy shirt. His heart squeezed as he realized it was one of the cashmere sweaters Bryson had bought him. Fuck it. He pulled it on along with the jeans and swiped some eyeliner on his lids. It wasn't great, but whatever. He just needed to get out of this house and away from Bryson.

He grabbed a black leather jacket and opened his bedroom door. Bryson stood on the other side, looking surprised to find himself face to face with King.

His gaze moved down King's body. "Are you going out?"

King thought about not responding. He wasn't on the clock. But his mouth couldn't stay silent when his heart hurt this badly. "Nothing is going on here, so I might as well."

Guilt flashed in Bryson's eyes. That doubled King's rage and pain. Bryson's open guilt proved he had known exactly what he was doing when he said those words, and he had done it anyhow. "I thought we were exclusive."

King fought a flinch. He wished he hadn't told Bryson about the club he had frequented before them. Bryson knew the place was a sex club filled with people ready to fuck anyone anywhere. "Oh. Are we exclusive? I thought you said we were nothing. I thought I was just some guy you're paying to fuck." King heard himself, but he was so damn mad. Not only had he let Bryson string him along and deny their relationship, Bryson also obviously hadn't listened earlier when King said he hadn't been with anyone else in ten years. Despite where he went, he wasn't that guy. But the moment Bryson saw him headed out, he assumed King would sleep with someone else. He assumed King was an easy fuck because he had been for Bryson. The deeper he fell down the rabbit hole of his thoughts, the uglier he felt inside. King hurt. He wanted to lash out. King wanted Bryson to feel the way he made King feel. While Bryson still reeled from King's last comment, King went for blood. "I've been paid to do a lot of things over the years, but this is the first time anyone has made me feel like this much of a whore. I may as well enjoy being one."

King pushed his way past Bryson, leaving him behind. He didn't look back. Fuck Bryson. He didn't love King. King was the same piece of meat up for auction he had always been. He needed to remember that.

Chapter Eight

The sun rose on a new day. King sat in his car inside the garage—where he had been all night—and stared at nothing. Maybe he had overreacted last night. He couldn't tell. King just loved Bryson so fucking much. He wanted Bryson to love him too. He had been so raw last night and had said things aloud he maybe wouldn't have otherwise. But maybe it wasn't as easy for Bryson to say things aloud, and maybe King should have shown him some grace.

Bryson hadn't dated a man before King. Being seen as gay was a huge leap for him. He wasn't just some guy. Bryson was special and his face was the face of his company. His private life could very well affect his company name. There would be people, especially in such a male-driven business, who wouldn't work with a gay man. They wouldn't care he was the best at what he did, because their bigotry would be bigger than their common sense.

The thing was, though, King also recognized that he wasn't wrong either. Bryson should have said all that to him and asked if King was okay with being a secret. He shouldn't have strung King along just because he could. King was so fucking in love with Bryson. He probably would have agreed to anything as long as they were together. But Bryson should have asked, and he didn't.

King opened his car door. One of them had to be willing to meet the other in the middle and talk about this. Thankfully, King hadn't left the house in his usual skirt and hose. He circled his car and popped the trunk. King kept a bag of clean men's clothing in his car just for these occasions. He peeled off the sweater and found a long sleeve shirt. With his shirt changed, he headed inside. Bryson would likely be eating breakfast by now. If he knew Kylian, he was still in bed or already making plans to go see his friends. King might have a few minutes to talk to Bryson alone.

King headed inside and straight for the dining room. The scent of bacon and eggs filled the air. As he stepped inside the dining room, King froze. Kylian and Bryson sat at the table together. Bryson looked up from his plate. His eyes looked dead.

Kylian didn't look like himself either, but he flashed King a smile. "Good morning, King. Grab a plate and join us."

"Guards eat in the kitchen." Bryson's voice was cold and hard.

King fought the urge to cry as something inside him shriveled and died.

Kylian gasped. "Dad. What is wrong with you? King is family."

King swallowed past the lump in his throat. "It's fine. Mr. Long is right. I'm nothing." He turned to head back inside the kitchen.

"King, wait."

King paused with one foot inside the kitchen at Kylian's plea. He glanced over his shoulder. Bryson had his elbows on the table, holding up his bowed head.

Kylian shot to his feet and crossed the room. He linked his arm through King's and kept moving, saving King from staring at Bryson. "Today is your day off, right?"

King focused on Kylian. "Yes."

"Good. Let's go shopping. I've been so busy with school, I haven't had time to buy anyone's Christmas gift yet. I'd planned to ask one of the guards to go with me, but I'd rather go with a friend."

"Do you need me to drive you to Cheyenne's?"

Kylian snorted. "I meant you, silly. You're my friend."

The desire to cry doubled. His throat swelled. "Okay. Go do whatever you need to do, and I'll warm up the car."

Kylian made a dismissive gesture. "I'm good. I just need my shoes and coat."

Together, they headed for the mudroom. King stood still, trying not to think while Kylian found his shoes.

As Kylian pulled on his jacket, their gazes met. Kylian eyed him closer. "Are you wearing eyeliner?"

Fuck. "Yes."

A bright smile exploded across Kylian's face. "I love it. Very sexy."

Despite the horrors of the past twelve hours, King smiled. "Thank you."

"Don't thank me. It's true. Are you ready?"

King nodded, and they headed for the garage.

Kylian motioned toward his red Jeep Wrangler. "I'll drive. My baby probably hasn't even been started since I've been gone."

King waited until they climbed inside to respond. "I've been moving her a few inches every couple of days for you. I didn't want your tires to get flat spots or your battery to die."

“Awww.” Kylian tossed a sweet smile his way. “It’s like you’re a second dad to me.”

The lump that lived in King’s throat doubled. That was what he wanted. He loved Kylian like a son. King had honestly believed they were headed toward being a real family. No one understood. He needed them to be his family. That dream was dead now.

Kylian didn’t pull from the garage. “Can I ask you something?”

King pulled himself from his growing pain. “Sure.”

“Do you remember when you taught me how to defend myself?”

Okay. King didn’t know where this was headed. “Yes.”

"Do you think you could also teach me to fight?"

Everything inside King went on high alert. He forgot about his problems. "Is everything okay? Did something happen at school? Just give me a name." Even King heard the violent edge to his tone.

Kylian chuckled and patted his arm. "Everything is fine. I'm just on my own now and people aren't as nice as I hoped at Princeton."

"Is someone bullying you? Give me a name," King repeated.

Kylian snorted and shook his head. "It's not like that. I'm just realizing I maybe spent too many years being softer than I should've been." Kylian stared at nothing. "Being different isn't always easy."

A pain hit King square in the chest. That was a sentiment he understood more than most. “No. It isn’t.”

Kylian looked his way. He was more serious than King had ever seen him. “I want to be someone else. Someone people don’t see as weak.”

King thought his chest would cave. It was like Kylian looked into his soul. King felt like he stared in a mirror while looking at Kylian. “I love you. If I had a son, I’d want him to be exactly like you. If anyone sees you as weak, then they’re a fool. You’re the bravest person I know. But if you need to learn to fight just to know that you can, then of course I’ll teach you. I want you to feel as strong as you already are.”

A sweet smile touched Kylian's lips. "Thank you and I love you too. I'm sorry Dad was being an ass this morning. I don't know what's up with him today." Kylian eased forward and the garage door opened. He kept his gaze locked straight ahead as he maneuvered from the driveway. "Do you want to tell me?"

King lost the battle against massaging his chest. "There's nothing to tell on my end. As he said, I'm just a guard. I do as I'm told." Like that, all the warmth his soul had regained from talking to Kylian disappeared. His problems returned. King went back to feeling used and unloved. He forced himself to focus on Kylian. At least one of the Long men loved him. He would fixate on that for now. In a few hours, who knew? Maybe his heart would finally give out.

Because he hated himself and everything, Bryson cleaned. There wasn't much to do since housekeepers stayed on top of everything. Bryson rearranged his stuff instead. He kept one eye on the security monitors, expecting King would leave again at any minute. King hadn't come back with Kylian until two hours ago. They had stayed gone all day and half the night. Now Bryson waited for the inevitable. He knew King would go back to his club tonight. Bryson wanted to torture himself with the sight of King walking away from their love. He wondered if King would come back this time. Probably not. Likely, he would rather Archer killed him at this point than have to stay with someone who treated him the way Bryson did. Bryson felt sick. He didn't deserve him.

A quiet knock came from the other side of the door. Despite everything, a smile tugged at Bryson's lips. He knew that timid knock. Kylian had always knocked on his door exactly the same every time he had wanted to sleep with Daddy because there were monsters in his closet. Being with Kylian was exactly what he needed.

"Come in."

Kylian slipped into the room and closed the door behind him. He looked nervous. Bryson hadn't seen him this apprehensive in ages. Kylian had grown into more confidence than was possibly healthy.

"What's wrong, baby?"

Kylian twisted his fingers. "Please tell me what's going on between you and King. And don't say nothing. I'm not blind. He's part of the family and you were really mean to him this morning. He's been beyond upset all day. I don't like being in the dark, and all the tension is aggravating my ulcer."

Bryson bit back a sigh and sat on the edge of the loveseat. With his elbows on his knees, Bryson tried to think of how to respond. Kylian was right. He wanted to say it was nothing, but it wasn't, and he didn't have anyone to talk to about it. Not to mention, Kylian suffered from a lot of anxiety. Bryson couldn't make it worse by continuing to stay silent. "I fucked up."

In a flash, Kylian was on the loveseat next to him, turned sideways, and with his knees drawn up to his chest. He looked ready to listen. “Go on.”

Bryson leaned back and blew out a sigh. “There’s not much to tell, really. Last night, when you walked into the kitchen and asked what was going on, and I said nothing, that was the wrong choice. Something was going on.”

Kylian nodded. “You two are dating. I know. I’m not blind. So, why are you ashamed of him?”

Pain slammed into his chest. Bryson covered his face for a second before dropping his hands. Apparently, King was right. He had come off as being ashamed. “I’m not, but I panicked and said the first thing that came to mind. King also accused me of being embarrassed by him and lashed out at me, saying some shit that hurt my feelings, and I don't know."

"You decided to keep hurting him in return."

Bryson didn't know what to say. It seemed he had done that. Bryson stared at the floor. He didn't know why he hadn't just let things go. Bryson had deserved King's anger. Pride, he supposed. That was always his downfall.

Kylian didn't make him feel better. "I don't understand. You love him. That's obvious to anyone who sees you two together. He looks at you when you're not looking. You stare at him every time he looks away. He's me, Dad." Bryson looked Kylian's way at the claim. There were tears in Kylian's eyes. "You saved me from a horrible existence, and I know you would never, ever hurt me. Why would you hurt King? You have to know he's just like I was. I can see it when I look at him." Kylian blinked. A tear slid down his cheek. "He's waiting for someone to see past his walls and rescue him from whatever hell he's seen. You're not this man. Hurt people hurt people. Someone has to break the cycle."

Bryson swiped the tear from Kylian's cheek and hauled him into his arms. For a few minutes, they sat like that. "I'll miss this when you leave again. How did you turn out so smart and independent? I blinked, and you were a grown man."

A watery chuckle escaped Kylian. "It's time for you to focus on yourself for a while. You've spent too many years worrying about me."

That was his job. It was one he would do until his dying breath, without an ounce of regret. That was how long he would love King too. So, Bryson had to be the one to bridge the gap. Living without King was no option at all.

King paced his room for what felt like hours. When he couldn't stand another second of that, he started pulling out every item of clothing, shoes, and makeup that Bryson had ever bought him. He didn't stop there. It wasn't enough. He had to shed everything about himself that made him different. King didn't know what difference it would make. He just hadn't hated himself this much in a long time. The clothes made him feel free. That was an illusion. He needed to let go of the dream of acceptance, love, and whatever else he fucking thought he had. It was a painful dream. King needed to kill everything inside himself and go back to the harsh lessons he had learned as a child. Only killing his soul would give him peace.

With everything in a huge pile on the floor, King took off his necklace next. He dropped it on top of the clothes. That hurt. He was glad for it. The torture had been what killed his humanity once. King could do it again.

He dropped onto his ass next to the bed and opened the drawer on his nightstand. All his pill bottles were still inside, even though it had been months since he had taken a single one. King hadn't made any conscious decision to stop. He had simply been too happy to care about it. King hadn't wanted those good feelings dampened. Now, he wasn't sure what to do. There was nothing good left to feel.

One by one, he lined the bottles into perfect rows beside him on the floor. He desperately wanted to drown the hurt now, but that would defeat his plan to torture himself until he was dead inside. So he stared at the bottles while he moved a few of them a couple of centimeters, ensuring they were perfectly aligned.

The door opened. King rolled his eyes at the sight of Bryson. "Yes, master. Come on in. After all, it's your house and I'm no one."

Bryson eyed the perfectly aligned pill bottles next to King on the floor before he glanced toward the pile of things Bryson had bought him. "What are you doing?"

King leaned his head back against the bed and stared at the ceiling. It hurt too much to look at Bryson. "I would say nothing, but since you own me, I guess I have to answer. I'm trying to decide what to do next. Maybe I'll burn everything about me that embarrasses you," he said, motioning toward the pile of clothes. He set his hand on a pill bottle. "Or maybe I'll just take all these, since stopping after St Lucia didn't matter anyhow." King dropped his gaze to his knees. "Nothing matters, I guess. Loving you changed nothing. If anything, it made this life harder. A slave is a slave is a slave."

Bryson crossed the room and straddled King's lap on the floor before King knew what he would do. He swiped all the bottles aside before wrapping his arms around King's neck. "Look at me."

King didn't want to, but his chin still lifted. Meeting Bryson's stare hurt more than he could stand.

Bryson waited until he had King's attention. He held King's stare for a moment. Then his gaze moved over King's features.

"What?" King asked, sounding hostile. He didn't try to tone it down. He hurt too badly.

Bryson pressed a quick kiss to King's lips before he saw it coming. He stood and held his hand out to King. "Come on. Grab that pile of stuff and come with me."

King ignored his hand. "Do I have a choice?"

"No." Bryson sounded matter of fact. "But not because I'm your boss. Because I love you and you'll understand in a minute. Grab your things."

King latched on to that I love you and took Bryson's hand without thinking. He was too stunned to do anything else. Bryson helped him stand. King bent to scoop up what he could. Bryson motioned for King to hand him something. "Give me that necklace."

King passed it along.

Bryson stuffed it in his pocket and then grabbed the lingerie that fell when King's arms were too full. "Let's go." Bryson headed out the door and King followed, still reeling. When they reached Bryson's room, he opened the door and headed inside. King stayed on his heels.

Bryson opened one of the closet doors and pointed inside. "This one is yours. Dump that stuff inside somewhere."

King stood in the middle of the bedroom, holding his clothes and feeling like an idiot. "What?"

Bryson's eyebrows rose. "What do you mean what? This is your room now too. Oh, and you're fired."

Each second that passed, King's confusion grew. "I don't understand what's happening."

With a sigh, Bryson threw the lingerie he held inside the closet. He closed the distance between them and relieved King of the clothes he carried. Bryson tossed those inside too. He came back and stood toe to toe with King. While King watched, Bryson dug the necklace from his pocket and put back around King's neck.

"I'm sorry, I was an ass. When Kylian almost caught us, I said the first thing that came to mind only because I hadn't talked to Kylian about us yet. He's never seen me date anyone since I threw his mom out. It just felt like I should talk to him privately first, but I hadn't figured out where to start yet." He brushed his hands down King's chest after securing the necklace. "I'm not ashamed of you. In fact, I'm very much in love with you. I just felt a certain responsibility to my son and his feelings. But I shouldn't have worried because I know how much he loves you. What I should've done, from the day we got back from St Lucia, is this." Bryson took a step back and dropped to one knee as he pulled something from his pocket. He held out a ring. "I love you. Seriously. A lot. You're the greatest thing that's happened to me since the birth of my son. If you can find it in your heart to forgive me, and do me the honor of marrying me, I promise you'll never feel like a slave or unwanted or anything bad ever again."

Shock resonated to the bottom of King's soul. A dozen things occurred to him at once. Bryson knew all King's secrets, and—until only moments earlier—still thought King was an addict. Yet he had still bought a ring with every intention of marrying King. What a dumbass. Thank god. "Yes. Absolutely."

A smile exploded across Bryson's face. He shot to his feet. Bryson slid the ring on King's finger. King didn't even look at it. He couldn't stop staring at Bryson's face. "I love you."

Bryson's gaze moved his way. His features softened. "I love you too."

King couldn't leave it at that. His words weren't nearly enough. "I love Kylian too. I want him to be my son. He feels like mine."

Unexpectedly, tears filled Bryson's eyes. He looked away and blinked, as if he couldn't take King staring at him while his emotions surged. Bryson cleared his throat. "He's grown, so that's up to him." He met King's stare again. "But I know he loves you and he was really upset with me about this morning. I can't tell you how sorry I am."

"We both said shit that we didn't mean."

Bryson chewed his bottom lip. "It killed me for you to go to the club last night." He visibly swallowed hard. "I know you like to watch, and I can't give you that."

King cupped Bryson's face and forced him to hold his stare. "There's nothing I want more than you. There's nothing I can't have with you and you alone. I didn't go out. I sat in my car all night and broke my own heart, thinking about how you didn't really want me. It's not in me to do anything that might hurt you." King shuffled even closer. He had a fear of his own he needed to address. "Don't hire another guard. You don't have to pay me or release me from my contract, but

I don't want anyone else watching you. That's my place."

A sweet smile touched Bryson's lips. "Baby, you've always been free of your contract. I would never keep you like you're some sort of slave. You also won't need me to pay you. Everything that's mine is yours. But if you want to be the one who always watches me, then that's fine. I kind of like staring at your sexy booty all the time like some sort of crazed pervert."

King didn't smile at Bryson's joke. He was too busy falling into Bryson's eyes. "I'm scarily obsessed with you. When I came back inside this morning, I was more than willing to drop at your feet and let you walk on me. It's honestly a little terrifying how much I'll endure just to be with you."

Bryson's smile fell. "I promise you'll be happy with me. Despite the way I acted last night, I swear it. No walking on you... unless you're into that."

A smile exploded across King's face. He grabbed Bryson's ass and lifted him off the floor. King headed for the bed, holding Bryson's stare. "I'll be the best husband. You'll see. You can put your feet wherever you want on my body, even if they're cold."

Bryson's goofy smile warmed King's heart. "Wow. You really must love me."

King stopped at the edge of the bed. "I really do. You're my whole world."

A quiet knock landed on the door. King and Bryson flashed each other a huge grin.

"That sounds like the other half of my universe."

Bryson's eyes turned misty again. "Thank you for saying that."

There was no need to thank him. King really felt that way. He set Bryson on his feet. "Come in," they yelled simultaneously.

Kylian peeked his head in the door. He wore a unicorn onesie. "Is everyone decent?"

"Yep," Bryson said, answering for them both.

Kylian stepped farther into the room. "Can I sleep with you two? There are monsters in my closet."

"Of course," they answered at the same time.

King moved to close the closet door while Bryson turned down the bed. Bryson turned off the lights and left the bathroom door cracked so a small amount of light would filter into the room. The three of them climbed into bed with Kylian in the middle. King and Bryson stared at each other across Kylian's body.

"When are you two getting married?"

King and Bryson shared a smile. Bryson answered. "As soon as I can rush King to the altar. Is that okay with you?"

Kylian nodded. "As long as I get to be there. I love you guys."

"I love you too," Bryson and King said simultaneously again.

They spent a few more minutes just cuddling together before King broke. "You'd tell me if something was wrong, right?"

Kylian didn't answer right away. Finally, he nodded. "Of course."

King had a bad feeling that wasn't true, but they had time. Soon enough, King would make Bryson and Kylian see. He would always take care of them. No matter the situation. He was theirs now in a way he had never belonged to anyone. King would die for them.

CHAPTER NINE

THEY WAITED UNTIL KYLIAN'S spring break to tie the knot. The three months also gave Bryson time to throw King the huge wedding he deserved. While King had insisted many times he didn't need anything big, Bryson needed to show the world his gorgeous man. Not only that, whether or not King admitted it, this extremely public claiming mattered to King. King had spent his entire life feeling unloved and unwanted. Bryson needed him to know things weren't like that anymore. He had found a permanent home and family. King's friend, Nebraska, had stood as King's best man. Nebraska had married Archer's personal bodyguard. The guy looked no older than Kylian, but Bryson was glad he came. It had been adorable to see the way King lit at the sight of him. King had confessed Nebraska was the only person, other than Bryson, who knew about his secret life. Bryson felt like that gave them an immediate connection. Archer and his husband Angel had also shown for the occasion. To Bryson's surprise, Archer was oddly friendly. Kylian had eyed the guy a little too closely for Bryson's comfort. Sometimes, Bryson worried Kylian knew more about Bryson's business than he let on. Still, the day had been perfect.

Bryson held his breath as he watched King unwrap their wedding gifts. He was obviously uncomfortable with the audience. Bryson had helped as much as possible so King wouldn't feel like he was the only center of attention. But when they reached their gift from Kylian, Bryson backed away. This one was just for King, and Bryson already knew what was inside.

King made a show of gently removing the bow. Bryson couldn't stop smiling while watching him. Not only was he on cloud nine about King being his husband, but it was also adorable the way King was so tender with the gift. He could be ruthless, but with Bryson and Kylian, he was a gentle giant. King finally managed to open the box without ripping anything.

Kylian practically danced in place with impatience.

King finally brushed aside the tissue paper. His forehead furrowed. "What's this?" He dug out the stack of papers inside. Kylian watched with his bottom lip between his teeth as King's gaze moved across the paper. King's chin shot up. His gaze landed on Kylian. "Are you serious?"

Kylian nodded. It was obvious he tried not to look hopeful.

King turned away and swiped at his eyes.

Everyone looked confused.

King turned back. He wasn't trying to hide his tears any longer. "You really want me to adopt you?"

Kylian nodded. His eyes welled with tears.

King circled the table. “Of course, baby.” He pulled Kylian into his arms. “There’s nothing I’d rather do than be your second dad.”

“I love you.” Kylian’s muffled words sounded against King’s chest.

King kissed his temple. “I love you too.”

The crowd murmured their approval, sounding moved. Bryson swiped at his eyes. His throat swelled. He had never dreamed he would have this life. Bryson had stayed single for years, because only this would do for his son. Kylian deserved a real second parent who loved him. That was King. King loved them the way they deserved. Bryson couldn’t wait any longer. He joined their hug. They sniffed and giggled in their tiny family pod. Bryson had never been happier. He couldn't wait for this to be the rest of his life.

King was an overwhelmed emotional wreck. Everything about the day had been flawless and his heart was too full. He couldn't stop staring at copies of all the papers he had signed. They were officially married, and he was now Kylian's dad. Not just stepfather, but dad. He hadn't expected that one, but he had signed immediately, and the paperwork had been whisked away by Bryson's attorney for immediate filing. King had been handed copies of everything and here they were: a real family.

They weren't leaving for their honeymoon until after Kylian returned to school. It was more important to spend as much time with him as possible. The bungalow Bryson had purchased in St. Lucia would still be there. King finally set the paperwork aside and rolled Bryson's way. They stared at each other from their pillows. On their sides, their fingers linked, while they silently held each other's gaze. Neither of them made a sound. Sometimes, there was nothing to say. They simply enjoyed existing together while knowing it had been the greatest day for them.

Bryson was the first one to scoot closer. King grabbed his waist and dragged him the final few inches. The bright smile Bryson wore was everything. "It was a great day, wasn't it?"

King nodded. “Perfect.” He swiped his lips across Bryson’s. “You looked so beautiful standing at that altar. I thought my heart would stop before we exchanged vows.”

Bryson leaned his head back an inch so he could hold King’s stare. “You looked amazing too, but I still wish you would’ve felt safe enough with me to wear the wedding dress I bought you.”

A pang of guilt hit King. Bryson had designed him a special wedding dress with the top half as a tux and the bottom half as a wedding dress with a long train. It was beautiful, but the thought of embarrassing Bryson had stopped King from wearing it at such a huge event.

King bit his bottom lip. He felt guilty and couldn’t wait any longer. “Damn. Since you're determined to ruin my surprise, I set up something for you for when we get to St. Lucia."

Happiness shone brightly in Bryson's eyes. "What?"

There was nothing left to do but spill. "Kylian is going with us for a couple of days so we can have a second, private ceremony. I plan to wear the dress."

"Are you serious?"

The excitement in Bryson's voice made King wish he had worn the dress today. It was just such a private thing to him. The way he dressed at night had always been something just for him, and for Bryson now. But obviously, this was important to Bryson too, so he had to do this. "Yep, I'm getting pretty for you on the beach."

"Yay." Bryson whispered the cheer.

King couldn't stop smiling. "I love you so much. I want you to have everything."

Bryson stroked King's chest. "I have everything right here. But I'm still super-duper excited to see you in that dress."

King swept his hand down Bryson's body. "I'm super-duper excited to see you in nothing afterward."

"You're seeing me in nothing right now."

A wicked chuckle rumbled from King's throat. He kept moving until he straddled Bryson's body. "I'll never have seen you enough. Looking at you, that saved me. I've spent so much time staring and memorizing. I don't know what sort of insanity made you decide to marry me, but damn. You're my everything."

Bryson stared at King with his heart in his eyes. "You weren't the only one who was saved. In every way, you're my hero. You've literally kept me alive. There's no one out there who could compete. No one else could love me the way you do. I would've been a fool to choose anyone else." Bryson's voice cracked. "I would die if I lost you."

"It'll never happen." King touched his lips to Bryson's and he doubled down on the vow inside his head. Bryson was his now. Whatever it took, King would keep Bryson safe until they died together in their nineties, holding hands. That was a promise. If he could make Bryson love him by sheer longing alone, he could make that vow come true too, and he would. Whoever was out there, still gunning for Bryson, they didn't stand a chance. King would tear the world apart for his husband. Nothing could stop their happily ever after.

Keep an eye out for the next Damaged Devils, *Unmatched Devil.*

Please consider leaving a review at the retailer where you purchased this book. Reviews really help with a book's visibility, which allows me to continue writing more stories. Thank you, Charity.

About the Author

Charity Parkerson is an award-winning and multi-published author with several companies. Born with no filter from her brain to her mouth, she decided to take this odd quirk and insert it in her characters. One of her greatest loves is writing morally gray characters. You'll find them scattered throughout her hundreds of titles.

*Eight-time Readers' Favorite Award Winner

*2015 Passionate Plume Award Finalist

*2013 Reviewers' Choice Award Winner

*2012 ARRA Finalist for Favorite Paranormal Romance

*Five-time winner of The Mistress of the Darkpath

Connect with her online:

*Sign up for her newsletter: https://sendfox.com/charityparkerson

*Join her readers' group on Facebook: http://bit.ly/CharitysTribe

*Website: https://www.charityparkerson.com

*A list of her social media accounts and giveaways all in one place: http://hy.page/charityparkerson

Content

Content Warning: Damaged Devils is a dark romance series that deals with dark subjects. There is murder, sexual assault, abuse, kidnapping, some dubcon, and power dynamic relationships. These are anti-hero books. They won't be for everyone.

www.ingramcontent.com/pod-product-compliance
Lightning Source LLC
La Vergne TN
LVHW010655110826
845149LV00014B/3105

* 9 7 8 1 9 5 9 5 7 6 2 3 5 *